THE BILLIONAIRE DADDY TEST

BILLIONAIRE ONLINE DATING SERIES BOOK #4

ELLE JAMES

TWISTED PAGE INC

THE BILLIONAIRE DADDY TEST

BILLIONAIRE ONLINE DATING SERIES
BOOK #4

New York Times & *USA Today*
Bestselling Author

ELLE JAMES

Dedicated to my husband for marrying a ready-made family and making it work. Our children learned a lot from you and are proud to call you Dad.

Elle James

AUTHOR'S NOTE

Billionaire Online Dating Service
The Billionaire Husband Test (#1)
The Billionaire Cinderella Test (#2)
The Billionaire Bride Test (#3)
The Billionaire Daddy Test (#4)
The Billionaire Matchmaker Test (#5)

Visit ellejames.com for more titles and release dates
For hot cowboys, visit her alter ego Myla Jackson at
mylajackson.com
and join Elle James and Myla Jackson's Newsletter at
Newsletter

CHAPTER 1

"JUST BECAUSE THREE of you have found the women of your dreams through BODS doesn't mean I will." Sean O'Leary tipped his bottle of beer back and took a long swallow.

"Leslie's dating system works," his friend Tag said. "You've got the proof right in front of you." He tipped his head toward the dance floor. "Have you ever seen Coop, Gage, or Moose happier than you see them now?"

Coop Johnson led his fiancée around the crowded floor of the Ugly Stick Saloon in a lively Texas Two-Step, smiling like a fool in love. In just a few short days, he would marry Emma and settle into his sprawling ranch house on his thousand-acre ranch, where they would live full, rich lives.

Not far behind him, Gage Tate and his fiancée,

1

Fiona McKenzie, twirled and nearly ran into Coop and Emma. The four of them laughed out loud.

Former model Jane Gentry, tried to keep superstar NFL football player Moose Smith from crashing into other dancers as they made their way around the floor.

Taggert Bronson sat beside Sean, his gaze on his friends, a smile pulling at his lips. "Yeah, Leslie has a gold mine in her system. We'll all be married before you know it."

Sean held up his hands. "Whoa, there. Who said I wanted to get married?"

Tag redirected his attention to Sean, a frown marring his brow. "Bud, every one of us made that vow all those years ago when we were so broke we didn't have a nickel to rub together between us."

"I agreed to the billionaire part, but I don't remember agreeing to the "being married with children" clause of that vow."

"What do you have against being married with children?" Tag said.

Sean stiffened. "I don't have anything against being married with children, as long as it's not me."

"Why not you?" Tag asked.

"I don't think I'd be good at it." He gave Tag the side-eye. "You met my father. He wasn't the best example."

"Sean," Tag leaned forward, setting down his empty beer bottle. "You're not your father."

2

"No, but why risk it?" He nodded toward their friends on the dance floor. "Leave the marriage and kids to the guys who are happy to jump in with both feet."

Tag shook his head. "You're missing out on a lifetime of love."

"Your opinion. Not mine."

"What opinion?" a female voice said from behind Sean. The woman at the root of all the happily-ever-afters pulled up a chair between Sean and Tag and set her wine glass on the table.

Tag leaned over and kissed her cheek. "Hey, beautiful."

She smiled. "Hey."

"Hi, Leslie," Sean said with a crooked grin.

"Hi, Sean." She smiled at him. "Sorry I'm late. I just hired an assistant and was showing her how to log onto the computer. It took longer than I expected." She raised an eyebrow and repeated, "What opinion? What's going on?"

"That Sean, here, is going to miss out on a lifetime of love if he doesn't marry and have kids," Tag said.

"Why are you so concerned about me getting married and having kids?" Sean waved at one of the waitresses and held up his empty beer bottle before he gave Tag a pointed stare. "I don't see you all fired up to try Leslie's service."

"I told you…I'm working on something I need to finish before I go searching for love on BODS." He winked at Leslie. "Besides, I know the system works. When I'm ready, I'll let you all know."

"Good," Leslie said. "You've been selling it to all your friends, and you haven't even tried it yourself."

"Right. You're not setting a good example, bro," Sean said. "And what's with the name? BODS." He shook his head. "Couldn't you come up with a better acronym?"

"If I get out of the billionaire business, I'll consider it," Leslie said. "In the meantime, it is what it is."

Tag chuckled. "And if it ain't broke, don't fix it." He winked at Leslie.

"What is it you don't like about the Billionaire Online Dating Service?" Leslie asked. "Is it the whole marriage thing? Or is it going on a blind date that bothers you most?"

Sean shrugged. "It might be both."

Leslie tilted her head to the side. "Explain."

"Frankly, I don't want to get married." Sean looked around the bar at the single women seated in clumps. "I don't mind a blind date. But what I *do* mind are unrealistic expectations. From my experience, most women are looking for a lasting relationship. I'm not."

"Is that why you haven't been dating for some time?" Tag asked.

"Yes." Sean said. He lifted his chin toward the

long, polished bar. "Take that little brunette sitting at the bar, sipping on a mixed drink. She's pretty. She looks like she'd be fun. I'd take her out once or twice. She'd start to get clingy. If we went on to the fifth or sixth date, she would expect me to put a ring on her finger."

"You don't know that," Leslie said. "There are many women who have opted to remain single. With the national average of marriages ending in divorce ranging between forty and fifty percent, many women would rather not marry and end up in a nasty divorce."

"You're not doing a very good job of selling your system," Sean said, a smile tugging at the corners of his lips.

Leslie raised an eyebrow. "If you recall, the name of the service is Billionaire Online Dating Service. It's designed to pair like-minded people. Not necessarily for marriage. Although that has been a happy result of the pairings." Leslie touched Sean's arm. "You can state plainly in the application that you do not intend to marry. There are plenty of women out there who have no intention of marrying, but who would like to date."

Sean brow furrowed. "You're telling me that these women actually put that in their profiles? That they don't want to marry?"

"Yes, that's exactly what I'm saying," Leslie said.

"The whole idea behind the service is to help line up a few dates with like-minded individuals."

Sean sat quietly, digesting Leslie's words. He'd thought all women wanted to get married and have babies. Preferably, before they got too old to conceive. "Are you serious? There are women among your clients who do not want to get hitched?"

"Absolutely," Leslie said. "It's one of the many questions we pose to clients. Then the service takes some of the guesswork out of finding a date. You put in your preferences, she puts in her preferences. If your preferences are a match and you like what you see on her profile, and she likes what she sees about yours, you communicate online. If the chat makes you want to meet each other, then you do. If it doesn't, you can keep looking."

"For other women who have no interest in getting married…?" Sean asked.

The waitress arrived with another long-neck bottle of beer, setting it on the table.

Sean snagged the bottle and tipped it up, swallowing half before he returned it to the table. "Still, I don't know if I want a computer setting me up on a blind date."

Leslie nodded toward the pretty brunette sitting at the bar. "If you prefer to take your chances by dating that woman sipping a fruity drink, by all means, go for it. You know nothing about her. She might be all into yoga and you might not be. She could be a vegetarian, while you like steak and lobster. She might be planning to marry and have four kids before she turns thirty." Leslie raised her eyebrows. "Again, you're taking your chances and wading into the unknown. With BODS, you at least get a few things clear before you even communicate for the first time…through an email or instant messaging. Your preference."

"You've heard Leslie's pitch on a number of occasions," Tag pointed out. "Weren't you listening?"

Sean's frown deepened, and he aimed it at Tag. "I heard."

"But were you listening?" Tag shook his head. "If you say you aren't interested in marriage, the women who are interested in marriage will not be interested in connecting."

"Exactly," Leslie said. "Only the women who are equally uninterested in marriage will."

Sean had a hard time wrapping his head around the fact that some women weren't interested in marriage.

"I can sign up for dating only?" Sean wanted to be perfectly clear.

"Yes," Leslie answered. "There really are women out there who only want to date."

Tag leaned toward his friend. "So, are you game for a go at BODS?"

Sean glared at Tag. "Don't push."

"The longer you wait, the smaller the pool of women your age who will be available," Tag reminded him.

"If it wasn't meant to be, I won't lose any sleep. Besides, I don't need a computer to find me a date."

"And you're back to taking your chances." Leslie smiled. "The brunette at the bar is smiling your way. Why don't you go ask her out?"

Sean considered the woman who smiled his way and flicked her hair back over her shoulder.

"She's interested." Leslie said. "You can tell by her body language."

Oh, her body was fine. But what language was she speaking?

Hey, darlin', wanna take me home and make love to me? After that, we can get married and have half a dozen children to trip over.

Sean shuddered and turned away from the brunette to face Leslie. "Are you sure there are women out there who aren't interested in getting married?"

She held up her hand as if swearing in court. "Positive."

"Fine. I'll be your next guinea pig."

Tag laughed and clapped a hand on his shoulder. "Believe me, brother, you won't regret it."

Sean scowled. "I'm beginning to regret it already."

. . .

"I MADE notes on everything you taught me yesterday. Right now, it's all scrambled in my head," Ava Swan said. "I want to do a good job for you. I don't want you to regret hiring me." She twisted her hands in her lap.

She hadn't had a new job in seven years. She'd worked for the same doctor's office all that time and knew the system inside and out. That job had been the one stable thing in her life when her world came crashing in around her. Unfortunately, that doctor had retired, and Ava had been forced to find new work.

"Ava, honey," Leslie said. "How long have we known each other?"

Ava gave her friend a shaky smile. "What, five years now?"

Leslie nodded her head. "I wouldn't have hired you, if I didn't think you could do the job."

"I know," Ava said. "I just don't want to disappoint you or mess up your new system. BODS is your baby, and I know how much it means to you."

"I built the program, making it pretty foolproof." Leslie pulled up a chair beside Ava. "The best way to learn the system is to fill it out like you were one of our clients."

"But I'm not a client," Ava said. "I have no intention of ever dating again. Especially, while Mica is young."

"Ava, it's been more than five years since your husband's death. Don't you think it's time that you started dating again?"

"I'm not ready for a relationship," Ava said.

"You don't need to be ready for a relationship," Leslie said. "But it wouldn't hurt to date."

"I don't know," Ava hedged. "I really don't want to bring a man into Mica's life. It would confuse her. And I don't want any man to assume the role of step-father. Been there, done that. I don't want Mica to have to go through what I did with my mother's second husband."

"So, you had a bad experience," Leslie said. "That doesn't mean every man will make a bad stepfather."

Ava shook her head. "I don't want to risk that kind of unhappiness with Mica." Ava twisted the ring on her finger. She still wore her wedding ring, even though it had been years since her husband's death. "It's bad enough that she's growing up without a father. I don't want to compound the problem by introducing a stepfather who doesn't love her."

Leslie leaned back in her chair and crossed her arms over her chest. "I get that you don't want to introduce a stepfather into your daughter's life. But aren't you lonely for some adult, male interaction?"

Ava's lips twisted into a smirk. "If you mean am I lonely for sex? Then the answer is no. I have BOB." Her cheeks heated at the admission.

"BOB?" Leslie frowned.

"Battery Operated Boyfriend," Ava said.

Leslie shook her head. "You have BOB, but is BOB enough?"

Ava shrugged. "He's enough."

"Does BOB take you out to dinner?" Leslie asked.

Ava frowned. "No."

"Does BOB talk to you and carry on a conversation that doesn't involve electronic humming?"

Ava squirmed in her chair. The intensity of Leslie's questioning brought back memories of sitting across the table from her husband.

They'd talked about politics, the weather, gossip, celebrities, music, movies and just about anything else. She missed that.

She missed him. Michael had been her first date, her first love, her high school sweetheart, and her husband. She'd never dated any other man.

She didn't know how.

Leslie took Ava's hand in hers. "You and I have belonged to the Get A Grip Grief Group for more than five years. We've seen so many of our friends in that group get on with their lives. Don't you think it's about time for you to get on with yours?"

Ava lifted a shoulder. "Maybe. But I really don't know how to date."

Leslie smiled. "All the more reason for you to get back out there and practice."

Ava's brow dipped. "Practice?"

Leslie nodded. "Yes, practice. You know, getting dressed up, wearing jewelry, applying date-night makeup, all the good stuff."

"But I already know how to do that," Ava insisted. "I get dressed every day to come to work. I wear makeup. What more is there?"

"Oh, honey..." Leslie clicked her tongue. "You dress like a mom."

Ava glanced down at her clothes. She liked her taupe-colored slacks, beige silk blouse and the matching beige cardigan. "What's wrong with what I'm wearing?"

Leslie's eyes opened wider. "Nothing's wrong with what you're wearing, if you only ever want to be known as Mica's mother."

"So, what's wrong with being known as Mica's mother?" Ava asked.

Leslie squeezed Ava's hand. "There's nothing wrong with being Mica's mother. You're a good mother to that child. But, you are more than just a mother. You're a beautiful, vibrant, exciting woman."

Ava snorted. "Darling, how much did you have to drink last night?"

"Not nearly enough," Leslie drawled.

"I'm not a beautiful, exciting, vibrant woman like you said," Ava said.

"Yes, you are." Leslie took her other hand in hers and squeezed hard. "You're beautiful. And, as much as you love your daughter, you need a life of your own."

"I have a life of my own." Ava smiled. "I work for you. I can get all the adult conversation I want when I'm at work."

Leslie shook her head. "It's not the same. You need *stimulating* conversation. With me, you're very comfortable, you can say anything, and it's just not enough."

"Yes, I *am* comfortable around you. And I feel like I can say anything that comes to my mind. You know me, and I know you." Ava held out her hands, palms up. "What's wrong with that?"

"That's just it; you need to get outside of your comfort zone," Leslie said.

Ava's frown deepened. "You're telling me I need to get *un*comfortable? How is that supposed to make me feel better about myself?"

"It'll make you more confident, more in control of your life."

"I don't need to date to feel in control," Ava said. "I have Mica. I'm the center of her existence. I control our lives together. And I have the most interesting conversations with her."

Leslie gave Ava a gentle smile. "Mica is an amazing little girl. She's smart as a whip, just like her mother. But she's not an adult, and she doesn't always ignite your mind the way you need."

"I don't know that I'm ready to do this." Ava

looked down at her hands. "Dating is so hard. Especially at my age. It's fine when you're young and don't know anything. But now... Well, I'm a mother. I've been married. I know what it's like to lose someone you love."

Leslie patted Ava's hands. "If you're going to work for me, you need to know what my clients are going through. It wouldn't be a bad idea for you to date, to give them an idea of what to expect."

Ava grimaced. "Oh right, make it a job requirement. Get to the girl that way." She raised an eyebrow. "That's playing dirty."

Leslie laughed. "Whatever it takes, girlfriend."

Ava pulled her hands from Leslie's grip and placed them on the keyboard of the computer in front of her. "Okay, boss. I'll consider this to be on-the-job training."

Leslie clapped her hands, grinning broadly. "Good. Then your first step is to fill out the form online. And by filling out the form, you will learn what our clients have to go through in order to be added to our database."

For the next hour, Ava and Leslie worked at the computer, entering Ava's information: her likes or dislikes, what she liked to eat, what kinds of physical activities she enjoyed and where she liked to go on vacation. When they were done entering all her preferences, Leslie made Ava take off her cardigan and stand by a ficus tree and smile while Leslie snapped a photograph of her.

Once they added the photograph to her profile, Leslie sat back and nodded toward the keyboard. "Now all you have to do is press enter. Once you press enter, your profile will be saved to the database."

Ava's finger hovered over the enter button on the keyboard. A combination of fear and excitement rippled through her.

"It's okay," Leslie said. "You don't have to date anyone you don't want to."

Ava gave her friend a weak smile. "Is it silly for me to think that by pushing this button, I could be changing my life?"

"It's not silly at all. We can only hope it changes your life." Leslie nodded. "Just do it."

Ava pressed enter. For a long moment, the screen seemed to be frozen. Ava held her breath, counting the seconds until the screen changed and a message popped up.

Congratulations! You have just taken the first step in finding your perfect match.

Ava's heart thumped against her ribs. "You know, I've been working for you for a whole two days, and I don't even know what BODS stands for."

Leslie laughed. "That's my fault. I should have made that clear upfront."

"I figure it has something to do with an online

dating system, but what does the B stand for?" Ava asked.

Leslie gave a somewhat secretive smile. "The B stands for best."

Ava nodded. She hoped Leslie was right. And she prayed she wouldn't regret having just entered her data into an online dating system.

CHAPTER 2

SEAN ENTERED the BODS office in downtown Austin, already regretting his decision to come. If his friend Tag hadn't insisted on accompanying him, he might not have come at all. At the very least, he might have turned around that moment and left before anyone saw him enter the office.

"I called ahead," Tag said. "Leslie is expecting us. Don't worry. It won't take long once you get started."

As they approached the reception desk, a brunette woman with brown eyes stood and smiled. "Hi, my name is Kayla. I'm the new temp. How can I help you?"

A door opened behind Kayla, and Leslie Lamb came out, wearing a soft gray business suit. Smiling, she rounded the desk and held out her hand to Sean. "I'm so glad you made it."

Sean pressed his lips firmly together. "I don't

think I had a choice." He tipped his head toward Tag. "My personal escort made sure I got here on time."

Leslie laughed. "I promise, it won't hurt a bit."

"I'll let you know." Sean shook Leslie's hand, and then studied the office.

The sitting area was furnished in light whites and grays—modern, but not uncomfortable. Sean had been here before with Coop, Gage and Moose, but he hadn't noted the décor. Now that it was *his* turn, he half-expected to walk into a very feminine boudoir with fuzzy pink heart-shaped pillows and photographs of kissing couples lining the walls.

The woman behind the desk smiled. "You must be our new client."

Sean's first thought was that Leslie had chosen well with her receptionist. The woman's voice was soft and husky and made him feel comfortable and welcome at the same time. Not to mention, she wasn't bad to look at, either.

However, Leslie's receptionist wasn't the reason why Sean was there.

"Leslie, do you want me to take our client back to the conference room?" the receptionist asked.

Leslie shook her head. "No, I'll handle this one myself." She glanced at Sean. "If you'll follow me."

Leslie led the way down a hall to a conference room where a computer sat at the end of one very long conference table.

"If you'll have a seat in front of the keyboard, I'll get you started, and then leave you alone to fill out the rest of the form on your own." Leslie pulled out a chair and waved her hand, indicating he should take it.

Sean shot a glance towards his friend Tag.

Tag nodded. "It's going to be all right. Leslie wouldn't lead you astray."

Leslie smiled. "Don't worry. You don't have to date anyone you don't want to."

"I'm not sure I want to date anyone at all," Sean said.

Leslie touched his arm. "Give it a chance."

"That's right, you have to give it a chance. You might be surprised by the outcome." Tag grinned.

"I don't like surprises," Sean said grumbled.

Leslie initiated the computer program, entered her password and brought up the first screen. "You start by entering the basic details: your name, age, height...you know, the usual stuff." You can enter a nickname, if you prefer not to use your formal first name. Most of your personal data will not be available to the applicants who are looking online. It's your preferences that they will have access to view. When you enter those, be sure to be honest and list things that are deal-breakers for you. Don't say things like 'I love romantic comedies,' if you'd rather stab yourself in the eye than watch one." Leslie smiled. "You want to attract somebody who will be attracted to you as you are, not as you think they want you to be."

"Trust me," Sean said, "I can be honest."

"Not brutally honest," Tag said. "You don't want to scare them away."

"Don't skimp on your preferences," Leslie said. "The more preferences you put down, the better the program can zero in on just the type of woman you would like to date." Leslie stood and smiled. "If you have any questions, I'll be in my office. All you have to do is come ask."

She hooked Tag's arm and practically dragged him out of the room.

"Shouldn't I help him go through his preferences?" Tag asked as Leslie closed the door between them and Sean.

Sean breathed a sigh of relief. At least he wouldn't have an audience witnessing his humiliation. He never would have pictured himself sitting in front of a computer monitor, filling out data for an online dating system at the ripe old age of thirty-three. Why was he here, anyway? He didn't need help finding a date.

But like Leslie said, when he went out with a woman he knew nothing about, he was taking his chances. She might be desperately seeking husband material. He was not husband material.

Sean sighed. What the heck? He might as well fill out the form. Like Tag said, he didn't have to date any of the women that came up on his profile. So, what would it hurt?

He started by entering his name and his nickname, Decker. Anonymity was important when you were a billionaire. It always seemed that when a woman found out that he was loaded, it changed her entire attitude toward him.

He'd rather meet someone who didn't know he had a loaded bank account, someone who liked seeing him, and who didn't mind watching a few football games. If she liked animals, and had actually ridden a horse more than once, all the better.

Sean leaned toward the computer and typed away.

"HOLY HECK, I don't have anything to wear." Ava riffled through her closet, desperately searching for something suitable to wear on a first date. She had no idea what a woman wore on such an occasion. She hadn't been on a date since high school. Surely, the rules changed from when one was a teenaged girl to a seasoned widow. "I can't believe I let you talk me into this."

"Calm down," Leslie said. "I have just what you need." She left the room. A moment later, the sound of the front door opening and closing indicated her friend had left the house.

"What am I supposed to do?" Ava cried to the

empty room, thankful the babysitter had taken Mica out to get dinner for the two of them.

The front door squeaked open and closed again, and Leslie was back in her bedroom carrying a garment bag.

When Leslie reentered the bedroom, Ava was holding her best beige dress and beige cardigan up to her chest.

Leslie came to a standstill, shaking her head. "No. You cannot go on a first date wearing that dress."

"It's the only dress I have that isn't stained or snagged."

"That's why you have friends." Leslie held up the garment bag with a smile. "Friends who bear gifts."

"You brought me a dress." Ava stared at Leslie, her eyes filling with grateful tears.

Leslie nodded. "Not only did I bring you a dress, I brought shoes and accessories to match."

"Well, don't just stand there, let's see what you've got. I only have fifteen minutes to get dressed, do my hair and makeup and get to the restaurant." Ava threw her hands in the air. "It's not going to happen. I shouldn't have gone to get my nails done. I knew it would take too long."

"You needed to have them done." Leslie snagged one of her hands and held it up, smiling. "Look how lovely they are."

They were perfect. Ava hadn't had her nails done

in… Well, too long for her to remember. Definitely pre-Mica.

"We don't have enough time. I'm going to be late," Ava wailed. Her first date in forever, and she couldn't even be on time. What would her date think of that? He'd think she didn't give a damn, or that she was rude and didn't respect him.

Leslie held up a hand. "No worries. We've got this. I can do your hair while you do your makeup. Once we have that done, you can dress. You're only ten minutes away from the restaurant. That gives us five minutes to work with. Let's get going."

She flung her hands in the air. "You can't do my hair in five minutes. It takes longer than that to brush out the tangles."

Leslie smiled confidently. "You will be amazed at what I can do in five minutes with a curling iron."

"What's the going grace period for being late on a first date," Ava asked. "Ten, maybe fifteen minutes tops?"

Leslie smiled. "Don't worry, he'll wait."

Ava dropped the beige dress onto the bed and raced to the bathroom, grabbed her hairbrush and yanked through the tangles.

She jerked open a drawer and sorted through it, trying to find her foundation. "Where's my foundation?" She yanked open another drawer. "I can't find it."

"Honey, you don't need base makeup. You have

perfect skin, your complexion is flawless," Leslie said. "What you need is smoky eyes."

"Smoky eyes?" Ava lifted her hands. She had no idea what Leslie was talking about. She'd been a mother for so long, and then before that, she'd dated her high school sweetheart. She didn't know a smoky eye from a can of tuna. "I'll be lucky just to get my mascara on without poking my eyes out."

"Give me your makeup," Leslie demanded.

"But if you do my makeup who's going to do my hair?" Ava despaired of getting to the restaurant within the next thirty minutes, much less than the fifteen she needed.

"Sweetie, it's going to be okay," Leslie said. "If you don't like him, you don't even have to stay."

"And that's supposed to make me feel better?" She grabbed her blush and a makeup brush and smoothed some of the powder on her cheeks. "What if he doesn't like me?"

Leslie shrugged. "You weren't interested in a lasting relationship, anyway. And you might get a free dinner out of this date. What have you got to lose?"

"Time with my daughter, my dignity." Ava blinked. "Hell, my sanity."

Leslie shook her head. "Close your eyes."

Ava stood with her eyes closed while Leslie applied shadow to her lids. At one point, she tried to turn toward the mirror.

Leslie directed her face back toward her. "You have to wait until I'm done."

After the shadow, her friend drew eyeliner at the base of Ava's eyelashes, and then dabbed on mascara. When she was done, she turned Ava toward the mirror and said, "Now, you can look."

Ava opened her eyes and blinked. "That's smoky eyes?"

Leslie nodded. "You look amazing. Now, let's apply some lipstick, do your hair and get you dressed."

Leslie pulled a tube of lipstick from her purse and smoothed it on Ava's lips. It was a bright cheery red and a color Ava would never have chosen for herself. But no other color would have complemented the smoky eyes as much.

With a hot curling iron, Leslie went to work on Ava's hair. A few short minutes later, Leslie had Ava's long blond hair tamed into soft curls, framing her face.

"Now, for the dress," Leslie said.

While Ava stripped out of her shorts and T shirt, Leslie unzipped the garment bag, pulled out and held up the shortest, sexiest little black dress Ava had ever seen.

She shook her head. "I can't wear that."

Lesley nodded and smiled. "Yes, you can."

"It's barely even a dress." Ava shook her head again. "It's more like a sleeve that goes on a dress."

Leslie laughed. "It's going to look fabulous on you."

Ava walk toward the bed where she'd thrown the beige dress and cardigan.

When she reached for it, Leslie slapped her hands away. "Oh, no you don't. The only place that dress is going is to the local women's shelter. No, make that to the local dump."

"You can't throw away my dress." Ava snatched it up and held it to her chest. "I don't have that many dresses in my closet."

Leslie pulled the dress from Ava's fingers. "Then wear jeans." She shoved the dress into her handbag and lifted the little black dress.

Ava backed away holding up her hands. "I can't wear that."

Leslie glanced down at her watch. "You have exactly one minute to get dressed and get out the door."

"One minute?" Ava squeaked.

Leslie shoved the black dress into Ava's hands.

Ava didn't have time to argue. She stepped into the dress and pulled it up over her hips and torso. Then she turned to let Leslie zip the back. When Ava faced her full-length mirror, she gasped at her reflection.

The black dress complemented her pale blond hair. The smoky eyes made her look mysterious, like somebody she didn't know, but wanted to.

Leslie stepped up behind her and laid her hands on her shoulders. "You look amazing."

"I don't know who that is," Ava said, staring at herself.

Leslie squeezed her shoulders. "You don't know who that is because you haven't been yourself since Mike died and you gave birth to Mica." She pressed a black clutch into Ava's hand. "Come on, I'm driving you to the restaurant."

"But I can drive myself. Besides, if I want to leave, I'll have my own vehicle there, and I can go whenever I need to."

Leslie smiled gently. "Take the risk, Ava." She touched a finger to the clutch. "Inside the clutch is your cellphone, some mad money, a key, a tube of lipstick and a condom."

Ava's jaw dropped. "I can't carry a condom to a first date."

Leslie nodded. "Yes, you can. The lipstick is for after the meal, so you still look good. The cellphone is for if you don't like him and you want to leave early—just call a cab. No worries. The key will get you back into the house. And the condom is if you really like him and things move along really quickly. You won't be unprotected."

Ava tried to push the clutch back into Leslie's hands. "No, no, I can't do this."

Leslie grabbed her elbow and steered her towards

the door. "You can, and you will. Now, let's hurry up. You're going to be late."

Leslie hustled her out to her sporty SUV and opened the passenger seat door for her to get in.

Ava would rather have driven her own vehicle, because at least then she would have been in control of something.

As it was, Leslie drove like a bat out of hell to get them to the restaurant only two minutes late. She pulled to a stop at the front door. "Okay, sweetie, have fun." She leaned across Ava and opened the passenger seat door, shoving it wide.

Ava hesitated. "That's it? That's all the advice I get?"

Leslie grinned "That's it. You're a grown woman. You can figure this out for yourself."

Ava eased out of the car, trying not to show too much leg or part of her bottom. "Thanks, I feel like you're throwing me into the deep end, and I don't know how to swim."

Leslie smiled. "You'll figure it out."

Ava watched as Leslie drove away, leaving her standing there all by herself in front of a restaurant where she was to meet a complete stranger and have dinner with someone she didn't know.

No stress. Nope. None.

Ava slowly walked toward the door and almost tripped over her own feet in the high heels Leslie had loaned her. She straightened and reach toward the door, pushing it inward.

She recognized the restaurant from the advertisements on television. It was an expensive steak restaurant. A place she'd never been because she couldn't afford it on her limited budget. She hoped like hell her date could afford it and didn't leave her washing dishes. She stepped up to the *maître d'*.

He nodded slightly and looked down his nose at her. "Do you have a reservation?"

Ava wanted to turn and run, but she didn't have her car and had no way to get her back to her house. Panic started to set in, until she reminded herself she had a cellphone. All she had to do was call a cab to come pick her up, which would take several long minutes.

She considered doing just that, but then she straightened her spine and smiled at the *maître d'*. "I don't have a reservation, but my date does. I'm to meet him at the bar."

The *maître d'* smiled. "If you will follow me, I will show you to the bar."

The deeper she went into the restaurant, the more committed she was to this first date with the stranger. Ava studied the people at the bar, looking for the face that she remembered from his profile.

None of the men looked like the man who called himself Sean Decker. Could it be that she was there first and that her date was late? Was he just as hesitant as she was to appear?

Ava thanked the *maître d'* and slipped onto a barstool. She wasn't very familiar with mixed drinks or different kinds of wines, so she ordered a drink she'd heard mentioned in movies. "I'll have a strawberry daiquiri," she said to the bartender.

The bartender mixed the drink and set it in front of her.

Thankfully, she couldn't taste the alcohol, and it was quite refreshing. Within moments, the alcohol helped calm her nerves.

One minute passed, then two, then three. After five minutes, she quit watching the door. What had Leslie said, fifteen minutes was the rule? Just ten minutes more, and she could leave.

"I TOLD you we'd be late if we stopped to pick up that kitten," Tag said.

Sean shook his head. "You wouldn't have left that kitten out in the middle of the road like that any more than I would."

Tag shrugged. "You're right. But it made us late."

"If she's my perfect match, like you say she is," Sean said, "she'll understand. In fact, she'll love kittens and wish I'd brought it to her."

Tag nodded. "Again, you're right."

"Only thing is," Sean's lips twisted, "what woman would believe that I stopped to pick up a kitten?"

Tag laughed. "That does sound like a pretty weak excuse. A made-up one at that."

"Do you see her yet?" Sean stared around the restaurant. Waiting in line for the *maître d'*, he took that moment to locate the face he'd only seen once online.

Tag tipped his head toward a table where a blonde sat alone. "Think that might be her?"

Sean shook his head. "Can't tell. Her back is to us."

The woman turned to look toward the door. She had to be at least in her fifties.

Sean frowned. "She's nice enough looking, but I don't think that woman is twenty-seven years old."

Tag tilted his head toward another blonde wearing a really short leopard-print skirt and a fuzzy pink tube top. She chewed gum smacking it loudly.

Sean shook his head. "I don't think so. If that's her, I'm turning around and leaving…no…running out of this restaurant."

Sean scanned the spacious room, searching for a bright blond head. When he didn't see anyone who fit the description or the picture that he'd seen on the internet, he turned to Tag. "I'm already ten minutes late. She probably gave up and thought I stood her up. You want to join me for dinner here, or would you rather go somewhere and get a burger and a beer?"

Tag stiffened and reached out to grip Sean's arm. "Whoa, cowboy, hold your horses. Do you see what I see?"

"Where?"

"Behind the tall man at the bar," Tag said. "Wait for it."

Sean turn the direction Tag indicated.

A tall man stood at the bar. When the bartender handed him his drink, he slipped into a barstool and rested his elbows on the counter. When he moved, Sean could see the woman seated behind him. The man who'd just taken his seat, spoke to her.

The woman gave him a brief smile and turned away. She obviously was not with the man.

"Wow, buddy. Are you seeing her?" Tag asked.

Sean's pulse quickened. Bright blond curls framed a beautiful face.

Her hair was perfect, her face was perfect, and she was dressed to the nines. She was beautiful, all right. And she had *high maintenance* written all over her.

Sean spun and headed for the exit.

Tag caught up with him and grabbed his arm. "Where you going?"

"She's not my type." Sean continued toward the exit.

Tag held onto his arm pulling him to a stop. "You don't know that until you meet her."

Sean turned back toward the blonde seated at the bar, toying with a frozen red drink.

"Look at her," Tag insisted.

"I did," Sean said. "She looks too high maintenance for me."

Tag waved his hand around the restaurant. "You chose the location. It's a high-end restaurant. Look at the people around you; they're dressed very nicely. At least she had the decency to wear appropriate clothing."

Sean glanced around at the other patrons of the establishment.

The women were dressed in very nice outfits, and the men wore suits and ties. Tag was right. His date was dressed appropriately for the location.

A wave of guilt washed over him. He'd almost made it out the door without meeting the woman. He would have been a huge cad if he had walked out and stood her up when she expected him to be there.

"I guess the least I can do is go introduce myself," Sean said.

Tag clapped his hand on his shoulder. "Now, you're talking."

Sean frowned at Tag. "You're not sticking around, are you?"

Tag shook his head. "Much as I'd like to stay and watch history in the making, I promised Leslie I'd go watch some romantic comedies with her."

Sean laughed. "Don't tell me you *like* romantic comedies."

Tag shook his head. "Not really. But I like it when Leslie laughs. That woman has a laugh."

Sean stared at his friend. "So, what's with you and Leslie anyway?"

Tag shook his head. "Nothing"

Sean thought there was more to *nothing* than Tag was letting on, but he had a date with the blonde sitting at the bar, and he didn't want to keep her waiting any longer. "Well, enjoy your romantic comedies with Leslie. I need to keep my date with the gorgeous blonde at the bar."

Tag grabbed his arm as he started toward the bar. "You did bring some condoms, didn't you?"

Sean stared at his friend. "This is a first date. What fool would think he'd have sex with his date on the first night out?"

Tag raise an eyebrow. "What fool would come unprepared if the opportunity came up?" He shrugged "Just saying."

Sean shook his head. "You can leave now."

"I'm out of here," Tag said as he turned and left.

Sean hesitated a moment longer. He did have a condom tucked into his wallet. Not that he expected an opportunity to arise in which he'd need it.

The woman at the bar opened her clutch, pulled out a cellphone, glanced at it and then stuck it back into her clutch and slid off the barstool.

Damn! He was late.

And she was leaving.

Sean crossed the floor in a few easy strides and stopped in front of the blonde as she tucked her clutch beneath her arm.

"Hi, you wouldn't happen to be Ava Swan, would you?" Sean asked.

The blonde glanced up at him, her eyes narrowing. "Who's asking?"

"I'm Sean O'Lear—Decker." Sean caught himself before he said his real name. "I'm your date."

She nodded. "I'm Ava. You're late. I was just leaving."

He smiled his most charming smile. The one that worked with every woman he'd ever known.

Apparently, it wasn't working with her.

"Please accept my apologies. I had to stop to rescue a kitten in the road." He knew the excuse sounded as made up as any. But damned if it wasn't the truth.

Her eyes narrowed even more. "Do you use that line with all your dates?"

Sean shook his head. "No, you're the first."

She wrinkled her brow. It was so cute when she did it, he wanted to lean over and kiss that eyebrow. The thought shocked him. He'd just met the woman, and already he was thinking about kissing her. Maybe Tag had it right when he'd asked him if he'd brought a condom along.

Ava's lips twisted into a wry smile. "I'll give you

points for the emotional impact of your story, but I'm not buying it."

"No, really, we had traffic backed up for over a mile on a six-lane road. All to save one tiny kitten who'd found its way out into the middle of a busy highway."

Ava shook her head. "I'm not inclined to believe you. But for the sake of my rumbling stomach, I'll give you the benefit of the doubt, this time. I might forgive your tardiness, but I'm not sure the *maître d'* will have held your table." She tipped her head toward the man guarding the entrance. Sean grinned. "I'll make it happen." He stared down at her. "So, you're staying?"

She smiled. "I came for the steak. It would be a shame to leave without it."

He chuckled. "I see where I rank."

She nodded. "Uh huh. Right after steak and wine. Only it might be wine, then steak, then you."

Sean held out his elbow. "I'll take it. At least I rank above dessert."

Ava tilted her head to the side and touched a finger to her chin. "Well, now that you mentioned it, it's steak then wine, then dessert, then you." She grinned and slipped her arm into the crook of his elbow.

He touched his free hand to his chest. "You hurt me, lady."

She snorted softly. "I'm sure you have thicker skin than that."

"You're right. It'll take a lot more than that to make me cry."

Sean escorted Ava to the table the *maître d'* indicated, all the while praying the pretty blonde wasn't an airhead, and that she could string words together in a sentence that didn't actually bore him to tears. So far, she had his attention. Hopefully, it would last.

As SEAN HELD the chair for her, Ava eased into the seat. She tugged at the hem of her dress, careful not to expose more than was already displayed of the long expanse of her bare legs. Once settled, she smiled up at him. "Thank you."

Sean took the seat across from her, unfolded his napkin and laid it across his lap.

The waiter appeared and handed them menus.

Ava stared at her menu, frowning.

"Is something wrong, madam?" the waiter asked.

"This menu doesn't list the prices," Ava noted and looked up.

"Mine does," Sean said.

"I don't understand." Ava turned over her menu, searching the back for the missing prices.

"I'm buying dinner. You don't need to worry about the prices," Sean said.

Ava's lips pressed into a line, but she didn't want to argue in front of the waiter.

"Madam, may I get you another strawberry daiquiri?" the waiter asked.

Ava grimaced. "No, thank you. What I would really like is a light beer."

"And you, sir?" The waiter waited for Sean's response.

"I'll have the same," he said.

After the waiter left with their drink order, Sean studied Ava. "Did you order a beer because you thought I would like one? Or because you actually like beer?"

Ava shuddered. "The strawberry daiquiri was okay at first, but after a while it was too sweet."

"Research has shown that our taste buds change approximately every seven years."

Ava nodded. "That would explain it. I don't eat a lot of sweets. It sets a bad example for M—others," she ended abruptly, having almost slipped up and mentioned her daughter.

"I haven't known too many women who appreciate a good beer," Sean said.

"I don't drink very often. But I remember enjoying an icy cold beer on a hot day when I was younger."

Sean smiled. "I find that refreshing, in a woman."

Her heart fluttered at his smile.

The waiter brought their beers and set them on the table.

Ava lifted her glass. "To getting to know each other."

"Right. To getting to know each other," he repeated and touched the rim of his glass to hers.

Then he waited while she took a long swallow from her glass.

The beer was better than the daiquiri, sliding down her throat, cool and refreshing, adding to the alcohol she'd already consumed in the mixed drink.

"Score one for the blonde," Sean muttered so low, Ava wasn't sure she'd heard him right.

He grinned and downed a long swallow of his own beer.

Ava set her glass on the table. "So, what made you think you needed an online dating system to get a date? I'm sure you don't have difficulty finding someone to go out with you."

Sean cocked an eyebrow. "I could ask the same thing."

Ava nodded. "For me, it was simple. It's been a long time since I had a date."

"That's hard to believe. You're a beautiful woman," Sean said.

"Thank you. But it's true. It's been a long time. I wasn't sure where to begin. Leslie's BODS system seemed like less of a shot in the dark. It gave me a chance to match my preferences before I actually agreed to a date."

Sean's lips quirked upward on the corners. "Sounds reasonable, maybe even logical."

Ava shrugged. "What about you? Did someone twist your arm."

Sean chuckled. "Actually, yes."

Ava's lips twisted into a wry smile. "And now, you're stuck with me."

Sean shook his head. "I wouldn't exactly call it stuck."

"You don't have to stay." Ava gave him a tight smile. "I'm sure you'd rather be anywhere other than sitting across a table from a woman you met online."

Her date frowned. Had the woman read his mind earlier? "I didn't say that."

Ava's smile broadened. "You didn't have to. To be honest, I felt the same way."

"Really?"

"As I'm sure you noticed in my profile, I've been married before," Ava said. "I have no intention of marrying again, at least, not anytime soon."

"Bad experience?

CHAPTER 3

"No. Exactly the opposite. I had a good marriage." She glanced down at her hands. Her finger where her ring had been still bore a white ring around it where her wedding ring had been until just before Leslie had arrived that evening.

"What happened?" Sean asked, his voice quieter than before.

"He died," she said, her tone flat, her lips pressing tightly together. "I have no desire to remarry."

"That's refreshing." Sean sighed. "Most women I date want only one thing. To put a ring on their finger. They want to get married."

Ava held up both hands. "Not me. In fact...in fact, I didn't even want to date."

"Then why are you here now?" he asked, his gaze curious.

Ava rolled her eyes. "A friend of mine said I needed to get out. That I was getting frumpy."

Sean gaze slipped over her from head to toe, lingering on her bare legs. "Sweetheart, you're anything but frumpy. I'd go so far as to say you're pretty damned hot."

Ava's cheeks heated. "Thank you. I'd like to take credit for that, but my friend loaned me the dress."

Sean smiled. "Your friend has good taste. You look amazing in that dress."

Her cheeks heated even more. "You're not just saying that to make me feel less awkward in a borrowed dress?"

He held up a hand like he was swearing on a bible in court. "I do so solemnly swear, you look amazing."

Ava held out her hand. "Now, if you'll let me at your menu, I'll get an idea of how far back I'll set your wallet."

Sean held the menu out of her reach. "I can afford anything you want on the menu. You don't have to worry that it will break me."

Ava's lips twisted. "It has been a long time since I've been on a date. I'm so used to paying my own way. The thought of someone else buying my dinner doesn't seem right. And I imagine most women are looking to get married." Ava shrugged. "Rest assured, I'm not most women."

Sean was beginning to believe that. He sat back in his chair and seemed to visibly relax. "I like a woman who is pretty straightforward and doesn't mince words."

Ava nodded. "And I like the same in a man," Ava said. "As long as he's not rude when he's giving it to me straight."

Sean tipped his head. "Fair enough." He opened the menu. "Your profile stated you like steak."

"I do like a good steak," Ava said. "I don't have much opportunity to eat steak, but I like it."

"Again, it's refreshing to go out with a woman who doesn't want to go to a tofu bar."

Ava grimaced. "I wouldn't even know how to eat tofu." She sighed. "I really would feel better if I could see the menu with the prices."

Sean frowned. "Okay, but remember, I can afford this."

Ava nodded. "I get that. But what would you expect in return."

"Nothing but your company for dinner. And if you don't want to keep me company for dinner, I'll be okay with that, but you'll still get your steak."

Ava pulled her bottom lip between her teeth and chewed on it. "Are the prices that bad?"

Sean handed her the menu. "Depends on what you think is bad."

Her gaze landed on the first price, and she gasped. "I think this is bad."

"I wouldn't have brought you here if I couldn't afford it." Sean took the menu from her. Then he handed her the other menu. "Just pick what you want. I can afford it."

Ava's stomach churned at the thought of spending that much money on one meal when she could purchase an entire month's worth of groceries with that amount.

Sean reached across the table and covered her hand with his. "It's okay."

A spark sizzled through her at his touch. She gulped and focused on not making a fool of herself. "I'd rather go to a fast food restaurant," she said.

He shook his head. "How about I order for you? Just tell me how you like your steak."

Ava nodded. "I like it medium."

The waiter returned.

Sean placed the order.

Ava fiddled with the clutch Leslie had loaned her.

She wondered if she should have taken out her phone and called a cab to take her home where she belonged. It had been a long time since she'd been out to a steak house. She wondered if all steak houses had gotten as expensive as this one. Or if this particular restaurant was extremely high-end.

She glanced around at the patrons. Most dressed in fine clothing. Sean had better be able to pay for dinner, or she'd be doing dishes for the rest of her life to pay for their dinner.

"So, you're a football fan," Sean said.

Ava smiled, glad the conversation was turning

toward something she felt strongly about. "In college football, I'm a big Texas A&M fan. When it comes to NFL, I'm Cowboys, all the way. Gotta support my home state." Her cheeks heated, and she wondered if he'd think she was silly.

Sean grinned. "It's a good thing you're an Aggies fan. That was my alma mater."

Ava nodded. "I saw that in your profile."

"What about you?" Sean asked.

"I'm a graduate from a community college," she said. "I'm working on my bachelor's degree in psychology. If all goes well, I hope to complete it within a year."

"What do you plan to do with the degree?"

She looked away, her thoughts on her future, which always seemed so far away when she was just trying to get by. So often, she felt like it was she and Mica against the world. "I want to help people who are suffering with Post Traumatic Stress." Her gaze returned to him.

He was staring at her, though he seemed to be looking through her to another time or place. Finally, he visibly shook himself and said, softly, "Lord knows, we need more people who understand PTSD."

"I know I have a long way to go to get through a masters and doctorate, but I have goals, and I'm pretty stubborn."

"I'm sure you'll make it. Through what university are you seeking your Bachelor's degree?" Sean asked.

"Texas A&M," she responded. "I'm doing most of my coursework online."

"It's a good school," he said.

"What did you study?" Ava asked.

"My degree is in business, with a minor in Military Science," Sean said.

Ava stiffened. "Were you a part of the Corps of Cadets?"

He nodded. "Yes, I was."

A chill feathered across her skin. "Did you serve any time on active duty?"

"Yes, I did." He frowned. "Is that a problem?"

Her lips thinned. "No."

"I served for six years on active duty and deployed twelve times as part of the US. Navy SEALs."

Her eyes rounded. "Wow. A Navy SEAL."

He nodded. "I qualified shortly after I entered active duty."

"I understand the training is pretty intense. Not many who start, finish. It takes someone special to make it all the way through," Ava said.

"I don't know about special." Sean grinned. "I guess you could say I'm stubborn."

"No doubt." Ava's hand tightened on the borrowed clutch. "Were you injured during that time?"

"Nothing major." His jaw firmed. "I was one of the

lucky ones. Some members of my team weren't nearly as fortunate. People I cared about were never really the same after they redeployed Stateside. They needed people like you, who were willing to help them understand and work through what they were feeling."

Ava studied Sean.

A shadow crossed over his face, and he turned away. "War has a way of changing a man."

"If you don't mind, I'd rather not talk about the war and military," Ava said. The memories associated with the discussion weren't all good. The one most prevalent was the one where the post chaplain had come to her with the news of her husband's death. She'd been so distraught, she'd almost lost the baby she'd been carrying in her belly. Her hand went to her now flat stomach.

"I agree. No more military talk." Sean gave her a tight smile. "What do you like to do for fun? I know our profiles list things we enjoy doing. Hearing it from you makes it more personal and less automated."

Ava straightened her shoulders and pasted a smile on her face. "I like to go for walks in the park." She didn't add that she liked to go to parks with playgrounds for Mica to play on.

Mica was a private part of her life that she didn't need to share on a first date. On any date, for that matter. Since she didn't plan on marrying again, at least until after Mica was old enough to be out on her own, she didn't need her daughter to be part of any conversation. She would never meet Ava's dates...if she should decide to go on more than this one.

"I like being outdoors, as well," Sean said. "Do you ride?"

"Ride what?" Ava frowned. "Motorcycles? No. Horses? I have."

Sean grinned. "Horses, although motorcycles can be fun, too."

"I've never been on a motorcycle, but I love riding horses. I had a friend in high school who would take me horseback riding every other weekend. I haven't been riding since then. There never seemed to be time or availability." She smiled across at him. "Life gets very busy when you're an adult."

"Great. I have horses," Sean said. "I love to ride. Unlike you, I didn't ride as a kid. I learned as an adult, after I left the Navy. If we agree to a second date, we might do it on horseback."

Riding horses reminded Ava of younger, carefree days. She smiled. "I'd like that."

Sean's brow wrinkled. "Like the idea of a second date? Or of doing it on horseback?"

"Both," she said, then blinked. She'd meant that.

Sean cocked an eyebrow. "You might want to hold your opinion until the end of the date. I might say something stupid that might change your mind about me."

Ava snorted softly. "Deal. I'll wait until the end of the evening to make my decision about you."

By the time she finished her beer, she had a little bit of a buzz, mellowing her nervousness.

They discussed the previous Aggie football season and the one upcoming in the fall. The conversation segued into a discussion about the different kinds of horses and places each had always want to go for trail riding, to include the Palo Duro Canyon in north Texas and the mining trails of Colorado.

Ava found herself relaxing and getting more comfortable with Sean. By the time their food came, he'd made her laugh twice.

Leslie had been right. She had needed adult, male conversation. And she was having fun.

The steak was so tender it practically melted in her mouth. She moaned her approval.

Sean chuckled. "I'm glad to see you appreciate a good steak."

"This is better than a good steak," she said. "And the asparagus is amazing."

Sean nodded. "They do a good job with the steaks here, but I still prefer homegrown beef, grilled on the barbeque out at the ranch. Nothing gets better."

Ava agreed. "There's something satisfying about grilling your own steak."

When they'd cleaned their plates, the w and took away their dishes. Then, he of the dessert menu.

Holding up her hand, Ava shook her head. "I couldn't fit another bite into this dress."

Sean thanked the waiter. "So, what next? Would you like to go dancing?"

Ava shook her head. "I shouldn't admit to this, but I don't usually stay up that late, unless I'm snuggled in a blanket on my couch, watching a good movie." She laughed. "Half the time, I fall asleep in the middle of it."

Tipping his head slightly, Sean studied her. "Most women would jump at the chance to go dancing."

Ava grinned. "We've already established that I'm not most women."

Sean nodded. "Right. It's just hard to get used to."

Ava tilted her head. "Do I detect a little cynicism toward the fair sex?"

His lips twisted wryly. "Guilty. You don't get to the ripe old age of thirty-three without going through a few bad dates that color your opinion."

"Well, I hope I'm not adding to your list of grievances."

He shook his head. "No way. So far, I'm intrigued." Sean glanced around. "If you don't want to go dancing, what would you like to do next?"

Ava gave him a smile. "I guess we could call it a night."

"How about this? Why don't we do a little window shopping. I'm not quite sure I'm ready to take you home." He tipped his head, his brow furrowing. "Unless you really want to go home now."

She wasn't ready to end the date. "I'm up for a little window shopping, if you are."

Sean paid the bill and held out his arm.

Ava slipped her hand through the crook of his elbow and let him guide her out of the restaurant. She felt almost comfortable with Sean. Not like she did with Leslie, but a little on the edge and relaxed all at once.

She was glad he let her hold onto his arm as they walked down the street. The borrowed shoes sported a heel a little higher than she was used to.

It was nice to have someone to lean on for a change. She had been leaned on for the past five years. It was nice to let someone else hold her up for a few minutes out of her life. Not that she planned on getting used to it.

This was just a date. She had no intention of taking it much farther than this one date. Okay, maybe she'd go for a second date. Ava frowned. If he asked.

She hoped he'd ask. He'd talked about going horseback riding. Would he ask again, and give her the option of saying yes or no?

Ava stewed on the possibilities.

"What's your preference? Country or city?" Sean asked, startling her out of her thoughts.

Ava tilted her head. "I like both. What I miss about

being in the country is being able to see the stars. My mother and I used to drive out to the country to see the meteor showers. When you're out in the Texas countryside, the sky is so wide open and full of stars, it's amazing. You can see all the meteors streaking through the heavens."

"I grew up in the city." Sean paused. "The only time I got to see the stars was when my brother and I drove out to the country to do a little illicit, underage drinking and raising hell."

Ava tilted her head and glanced up at Sean. "So, you had a little wild streak in you?"

"Yes, I guess I did." Sean gave her a crooked smile. "My dad wasn't the best example a parent could set for his boys. You see, he was an alcoholic."

Ava nodded. "I'm sorry to hear that."

"Please, don't let that influence your opinion of me. We don't get to choose our parents." Sean drew in a deep breath and let it out. "I've spent a lifetime overcoming my upbringing."

Ava smiled. "From what little I've seen so far, you appear to have succeeded."

They walked along in silence, glancing into store windows, until Sean brought them to a halt in front of a large pickup with knobby tires.

Sean waved a hand at it. "This is mine. I forgot to ask if you drove your own vehicle to the restaurant."

"No," Ava said. "My friend, Leslie, dropped me off."

He frowned. "Leslie, as in BODS Leslie?"

Ava dipped her head. "She's also my boss."

Sean smiled. "She roped you into trying her system?"

Ava gave him a shy smile. "I'm glad she did."

"Me, too." Sean rested his hand on the truck's door handle. "Do you trust me to get you home safely?"

With a nod, Ava smiled. Though she'd only known him a short time, she felt she could trust him with her life. "I do. But if you're not going in my direction, I could catch a cab to get home."

Sean shook his head. "What kind of gentleman would I be, if I didn't offer you a ride home from our first date?"

She shrugged. "You are under no obligation to take me home. We went into this dating gig with the option of leaving, at a moment's notice, if we didn't click. If you didn't like me, you didn't have to stay for the rest of the date. If I didn't like you, I didn't have to stay."

He turned her toward him and stared down at her. "It might be too soon to say, but I kind of like you." Sean pushed a strand of her hair back behind her ear. "If you'll agree to it, I'd like to take you home."

She nodded, finding it difficult to make her tongue work when he touched her like that. She managed to say, "I'd like that."

He helped her into the truck, his hand lingering on hers.

That tingling awareness spread across her like wildfire. She fought to tamp down the flames and gave him her address.

Although it was only five minutes to get to her house, it was long enough for Ava to get nervous.

Since it had been a long time since she'd been out with a man, and they were both grown adults, not teenagers, she wasn't sure if kissing was something done on a first date. Didn't most dates end in a kiss? Did she want him to kiss her?

A tug deep down in her core answered for her. *Yes.*

CHAPTER 4

THE DRIVE WAS TOO SHORT. Sean needed another ten to fifteen minutes to work up the courage to kiss this woman who'd more or less told him she didn't want to date and had no intention of going after a lasting relationship.

So, why did he have this unwavering desire to kiss her? Was it because he and she were so much alike? It was positively frightening.

He almost laughed out loud at himself.

Him, a Navy SEAL, afraid of a woman?

He frowned as he pulled up to a quaint little cottage at the address she'd specified.

"I know it's small, but it's home," Ava said.

"It's cute," he remarked.

"You were frowning like you didn't like it."

Sean shook his head. "I was frowning because the evening is ending far too soon."

She grimaced. "Sorry. After working all week, I'm pretty beat on Friday nights."

"Don't be sorry. I have to admit, although I can cut a mean two-step, I wasn't feeling much like dancing, either." However, he didn't want her to go yet. He wanted to hold onto her a little longer.

Ava liked the things he liked, laughed at his jokes, and felt warm and soft when she leaned into him.

When she moved to open her own door, he reached for her arm and squeezed it gently. "Let me complete my gentlemanly duties. We can't let your first day back in the saddle of dating end in a fiery crash and burn." He winked and got out of the truck.

He opened her door, then reached up and caught her around her waist to help her to the ground, letting her body slide down the length of his.

Sean swallowed a groan as he continued to hold onto her waist, even though her feet were solidly on the pavement.

For a long moment, Ava stood with her hands pressed to his chest, staring up into his eyes. "You don't have to walk me to my door, you know."

"Yes, I do," he murmured, his head dipping low. If he lowered it any more, he could capture her lips with his and end the night on a kiss that would almost certainly rock his world.

A dog barked from a nearby backyard.

Ava's eyes widened, and she stepped out of his

grip. "I guess I'd better go inside before Georgie, my neighbor's black lab, disturbs the peace."

Before she could go too far, he captured her hand and fell in step beside her. "Thank you for going out with me tonight," he said.

"Thank you for not being a jerk," she said with a grin.

"Glad I could oblige," he said, touching two fingers to his forehead in a mock salute.

"I've heard horror stories from women I've known who jumped back into the dating scene and went with other match-making websites to find a date. It wasn't reassuring. I almost backed out at least a dozen times before I arrived at the restaurant."

"I'm glad you didn't. I had a surprisingly wonderful evening." He climbed the porch steps and stopped beside her at her front door.

"Well, I guess this is it."

He nodded. "I guess so."

She raised her head, but her gaze didn't make it to his eyes, stopping short around his mouth or chin.

What was she thinking? Was she ready to get away from him? If so, why? Had he not been attentive enough? Had he said something wrong?

He placed his finger beneath her chin and angled her face upward, letting the light over the door shine down into her eyes. "What's wrong?" he asked.

She laughed. "Nothing. Why did you think there was anything wrong?"

"You've been talking to me all evening, smiling and laughing. Since we drove up to your house, you haven't stopped frowning."

Her frown lifted, and her eyes rounded. "*You* were frowning. I thought you didn't like my little house."

"I like the outside." He leaned back and gave the house another look. "It reminds me of something..."

Her brow furrowed. "Yeah?"

He returned his attention to her. "It reminds me of home."

Her frown deepened. "Your home?"

"Not mine," he snorted. "The home I fantasized about as a kid."

She touched a hand to his chest. "I'm sorry."

He took one of her hands in his and brought it to his lips. "Don't feel sorry for me. All that fantasizing helped guide me into the future." He leaned close. "A future where I could stand on the front porch of a house I only dreamed about with a beautiful woman." He stared into her face, captivated by her clear blue eyes. Resistance was futile. He had to...kiss her.

Sean leaned down and claimed her mouth with his.

Ava stiffened for a moment, and then melted into him, her hands moving up to wrap around his neck. Her lips opened.

Sean slipped his tongue between her teeth and caressed hers, loving the taste, the texture and heat.

The light blinked on over their heads.

"Ms. Swan? Is that you?" a female voice called out.

Ava sighed and stepped out of Sean's arms. "Yes, Darcy. It's me," she answered.

The front door opened, and a young woman leaned out. "I thought you might have forgotten your keys." She spotted Sean, and her eyes rounded. "Oh. Sorry. Did I interrupt something?"

Ava's cheeks bloomed with color. "No, no. Mr. Decker was just leaving."

"Hi, Mr. Decker." The young woman held out her hand.

Sean took her hand.

"I'm Darcy," she said. "I'm the—"

Ava stepped between them, forcing Darcy to drop her hand. "Darcy, thank you for opening the door for me." She moved toward the door and stopped short when another face appeared in the crack.

Sean's heart skipped a few beats as he gazed down at the prettiest little girl he'd ever seen.

"Mica, darling." Ava knelt down in front of the little girl with vivid blue eyes and light blond hair curling around her face and shoulders. "Why are you still awake?"

"I was waiting for you." The little girl pushed past Darcy and flung her arms around Ava.

Ava scooped her up and held her tightly. "Hey, sweetie, I told you I was coming back late. You weren't supposed to wait up for me."

Mica buried her face in Ava's shoulder. "I know, but I couldn't sleep."

Ava leaned back and tipped Mica's face up to stare into her eyes. "Why not?"

"Someone has to read to me," she said, her gaze shifting to Sean.

He tensed.

"I offered to read to her, but she didn't want me," Darcy said.

Ava smiled at the young woman. "Thank you, Darcy. Is your boyfriend picking you up?"

She nodded. "I just texted him. He's not far from here. He should be here any second." Darcy grinned as headlights flashed at the end of the street. "That's him, now. I'll just grab my things." The young woman ducked back inside and returned, carrying a light-weight jacket and a crossbody purse. "See ya Monday," she said and ran down the driveway to the Ford Mustang sports car that pulled up against the curb.

The little girl clasped Ava's cheeks between her little hands and forced Ava to look at her. "Who is he?" she whispered, her gaze shooting to Sean.

Ava gave her a weak smile and set her on her feet. "This is a...friend of mine."

Sean smiled, feeling a little on the spot. "I'm Sean." He held out his hand.

Mica looked from Sean to Ava and back to Sean.

"It's okay," Ava said. "He just wants to shake your hand."

Mica took his hand and gave it a firm shake. Her warm hand in his felt so small and fragile. His hand completely engulfed hers. But she stood tall, her shoulders back and her chin held high. "Nice to meet you, Mister."

"Decker," Ava prompted. "Mr. Decker."

"Mr. Decker," Mica said. "Aren't you going to come inside?" She led the way to the door and held it open for Sean and Ava.

Ava frowned. "I'm sure Mr. Decker has to go, don't you?"

"Please, Mr. Decker," Mica turned those pretty blue eyes up at him. "Won't you read to me? At least the boy parts. Mama tries, but she doesn't sound like a boy."

Sean chuckled. "No, she doesn't." He caught Ava's glance. "I don't have to be anywhere else. Sure. Why not?" His brow dipped. "If that's okay with your mama." He raised an eyebrow, challenging Ava to say no or let him come in.

For a moment, she chewed on her lip, her frown deepening.

Not Mica. She hopped up and down, clapping her hands, a huge grin splitting her face. "Yay! I'll have two people reading to me tonight."

"I don't know, Mica. It's late."

"Just one story," she said. "Please." She looked up at her mother, her eyes wide, innocent and pleading.

"I don't know how you can say no to that," Sean said softly.

Ava's lips twisted. "It's not easy." She tilted her head. "I guess if you're okay with it, I am."

"I promise you can trust me."

"I know that," Ava said. "Leslie vets all of her clients. She wouldn't have added you to her database, if you hadn't passed her background check."

"She did a background check on me?" He chuckled.

Ava nodded. "It was in the fine print."

"Remind me to read fine print before signing another legal document."

"I will. But for now, we have a book to read. I guess you're covering all the boy parts."

Mica skipped ahead in her soft pink nightgown, her blond curls bouncing with every step. She led the way to a small bedroom in a short hallway. Inside was a full-sized bed with a swath of sheer, gauzy material hanging from the wall over the pillows.

"Do you like my princess bed?" Mica asked. "Mama made it for me. I love it." She moved around the room to a small teepee in the far corner. "And she made a teepee. Sometimes, I sleep in the teepee. But not tonight." She hopped up onto the bed and stacked her pillows against the padded headboard. One on each side.

Ava pulled a colorful book from a small white bookshelf and carried it to the bed.

Mica patted the mattress on one side of her. "You can sit here," she said to Sean.

Sean had thought he'd be sitting in a chair, but there wasn't one in the room. So, he sat on the bed beside Mica.

Ava sat on the other side of the little girl.

Looking at them side by side, Sean could see the striking resemblance. Mica was the spitting image of her mother. She would grow to be just as beautiful as Ava.

Something pulled hard in Sean's chest. He didn't have time to examine that feeling as Mica took the book from her mother's hands and handed it to Sean. "You can start."

"Oh, okay."

"You don't have to do it," Ava whispered over Mica's head.

Sean shook his head. "I want to." Then he opened the book and read a story about a little princess, a wizard and a pesky dragon.

Sean read the "boy" parts and Ava handled the "girl" parts of the story. By the time they reached the end of the short book, Mica's eyes were drooping, and she yawned.

Sean slipped off the bed and straightened.

"Go to sleep, little one." Ava tucked the blanket around her daughter and smiled down at her.

"Could I have a drink of water?" Mica asked and yawned again.

"Of course." Ava glanced at Sean. "I'll be right back."

Sean nodded. "I'll stick around."

Ava left the room and hurried down the hallway to the little kitchen.

"Mr. Decker," Mica lay with her head against her pillow, her eyes half-closed. "Thank you for reading to me."

"You're welcome," he said. He had never read to a child before. The act had been strangely gratifying.

"Mr. Decker?"

"Yes, Mica?"

Her eyes had closed all the way. "Will you be my daddy?" Mica whispered.

Sean's heart stopped for several beats and then raced away again. "Pardon me?"

"Will you be my…" Mica drew in a deep breath and yawned again. "Daddy?"

Oh, hell. What was he supposed to say? "Don't you have a daddy?"

She shook her head. "No, he died."

"I'm sorry to hear that," Sean said. And he really was. A little girl needed a *good* man in her life to guide and protect her. But she had Ava, and Ava was doing her best to give her little girl all the love and attention she deserved.

"Mr. Decker?" Mica opened her eyes and reached out a hand to Sean.

He crossed to her and took her hand. "Yes, Mica?"

"They're having Daddy Day at school on Monday," she said. "Will you be my daddy?"

"Mica, I'm not your daddy." He hated disappointing the child, but it didn't seem right for him to pretend to be something he wasn't.

She gave him the saddest look that hit him square in the heart. "I don't know any other men. Except Mr. Johnson, the janitor, and he's old enough to be a grandpa. I want someone to be my daddy for Daddy Day. All the other children's daddies are coming."

"Can't your mother come instead?" he asked, feeling himself get sucked into those watery blue eyes.

She shook her head. "She's not a daddy. It's only for daddies. If I don't have a daddy, I have to sit by myself." She took his hand in both of hers. "Please, Mr. Decker. Will you be my daddy, just for Daddy Day?"

He couldn't look into that little girl's eyes and say no. She had tears brimming and her little hands holding his squeezed hard is if trying to squeeze a yes out of him.

When he opened his mouth to say no, a different word came out. "Okay."

Her eyes widened, and a smile spread across her face. That smile lit the room with her joy. "You will?"

She pressed a kiss to the back of his hand. "Thank you, Mr. Decker. Thank you so very much."

"You'll have to tell your mother. She might not want me to go."

"I'll tell her." Mica said. "I can't wait for Monday. I'm going to have a daddy at Daddy Day for the first time ever."

Her words tugged at Sean's heart again. He shouldn't have said yes, but he couldn't disappoint her. She so desperately wanted to participate in Daddy Day with a daddy of her own, even if he really wasn't her daddy. At least for a day, she'd be like all the other kids who had fathers who loved them.

Sean leaned down and pressed a kiss to Mica's forehead. "I'd better go."

"You'll be at my school at ten o'clock on Monday?" She named the school and waited for his response.

"I'll be there," he promised. "Now, you need to sleep. It's late."

"I will. I'll go right to sleep. I'm a very good girl. And you'll be a very good daddy." She turned on her side, closed her eyes and pulled a stuffed bunny up to her cheek. "Thank you, Mr. Decker. I'll love having you as a daddy."

Sean backed out of the room, wondering if he'd just agreed to something he shouldn't have. He didn't want to set Mica up for future disappointment.

It was only one day. How much could that hurt?

Surely, she wouldn't expect anything more from him. Would she?

"Did I miss anything?" Ava hurried down the hallway carrying a plastic cup of water. "My sink sprang a leak. I had to find a bucket to catch the water and clean up the mess.

She wore an apron over the little black dress, and she'd shed her high heeled shoes somewhere along the way, making her considerably shorter than the woman he'd met in the restaurant. Ava was a petite little thing, the kind of woman a man wanted to protect.

"What's leaking?" he asked.

"The drain beneath the sink," she said. "I'll have to call a plumber tomorrow. I put a pan beneath it for now. It'll be fine."

Sean frowned. "I'll take a look at it."

"Oh, no. You'll get your clothes all wet. I was lucky enough to find this old apron to cover the dress Leslie loaned me." She smiled. "Thank you, but you don't have to do anything with my old drain." She glanced down at the cup in her hand. "Let me give this to Mica, then I'll walk you to the door."

He waited for her to enter Mica's room. While she was saying goodnight to her daughter, he walked down the hallway to the small kitchen. The floor was damp where she'd mopped up the water.

Sean slipped the suit jacket from his shoulder and rolled up his sleeves. It had been a while since he'd done any plumbing, but he'd worked his way through college. One of his jobs had been assisting a construction crew. He had installed his share of sinks in the past and understood how they worked.

He found a couple of dish towels and spread them out over the damp floor. Once he had the floor relatively covered, he laid down on his back, reached under the sink and jiggled the drainpipes, searching for anything loose.

He tightened one of the connections and looked over the rest of the pipes. They appeared to be intact and working appropriately.

"Sean? Seriously, you shouldn't be working on my plumbing." Ava hurried into the kitchen.

"While you're up there, would you turn on the water. I want to see if it's still leaking."

"Are you sure? It was pouring out pretty steady when I turned it on just a minute ago."

"I'm sure," he said. To be safe, he backed out of the cabinet and sat cross-legged.

Ava turned on the water and bent to watch as it slid down through the drain.

Nothing dripped or gushed.

She grinned and extended a hand, pulling him to his feet. "You just saved my next paycheck."

"Glad I could help." Hell, if one visit from a plumber set her back an entire paycheck, she wasn't making much. Which would account for the small house in an older neighborhood. He wanted to do more, but it wasn't his place to. They'd only been out on one date.

She walked with him to the front door. "Look. I'm sorry your evening ended with you having to fix my sink and read a story to my daughter. I'm pretty sure that wasn't how you pictured spending your evening."

"Actually, I enjoyed myself, more than I thought I would."

"Really?" She grimaced and lowered her voice to a whisper. "I hadn't planned on introducing you to Mica. She's the main reason I haven't dated since my husband's death."

"Mica's a wonderful little girl."

Ava smiled. "I know. I just hadn't planned on dating again until she was grown and on her own. I didn't want to confuse her by bringing other men into her life. I think most men shy away from ready-made families, and I don't want her to get attached to someone who isn't going to be around for the long haul." She sighed.

"So, we messed up tonight."

Ava nodded. "She was supposed to be asleep when I got home."

"Instead, she met the man." He jabbed a thumb at his chest.

"Yes." Ava sighed. "She's been noticing other children have daddies and she doesn't. She never even knew her father. He died when I was pregnant with

Mica." A shadow crossed her face. "He was so excited to be a father."

"I'm sorry for your loss. And for Mica's."

"Michael would have been a good father. So, you see, I don't want to bring another man into Mica's life who won't love her as much as she deserves." Ava squared her shoulders. "So, you see now why I'm not looking for a relationship. I want to protect Mica from disappointment."

"I get that," he said. "But there are men out there who have done a great job of raising children who aren't their own. Being related doesn't guarantee a man will make a good father. My father was a prime example. I don't think he ever cared about me or my brother. He thought we were put on the earth to aggravate him."

"I'm so sorry." She touched his arm. "No child should feel that unloved."

"Yeah. Well, I survived, but I didn't have the best role model. If genetics has any say in my personality, I won't make much of a father. I don't even want to risk it."

Ava frowned. "You aren't your father."

"No, I'm not. And I'd better get going. I've kept you up past your bedtime." He smiled and touched a hand to her cheek. "Thank you for going out with me."

"No, thank you, despite how it ended." She cupped

his hand on her face. "I'd like to make it up to you, though, if I could. I can't afford to take you out to that fancy steak house, but I'm a pretty decent cook. Will you let me make dinner for you sometime?" She released his hand and stepped back. "You're under no obligation, and you know I have no expectations of anything. And you don't have to say yes."

He pressed a finger to her lips. "It's okay. I'd like to have dinner with you again."

"I have a friend who could keep Mica while we have dinner, unless you want me to cook it at your place?"

"Here would be fine. And it's Mica's home. You shouldn't have to boot her for me."

Ava chewed on her bottom lip before continuing. "She'd love it, but, like I said, I don't want to confuse her by bringing someone into her life who won't be around for the long haul."

Sean nodded and held up a finger. "I get it. And based on that thought, I have a confession to make."

Ava's brow dipped. "Confession?"

He nodded. "While you were wrestling the sink, Mica asked me to attend a function with her at her school."

"What?" Ava's frown deepened. "What function?"

"Apparently, they're having Daddy Day on Monday."

"How did I not know about this?" Ava shook her

head. "She usually tells me everything. And I get flyers from the school on all major events."

"Maybe she didn't want to tell you because it would make you feel bad? I don't know." Sean pushed a hand through his hair. "All I know is that she asked me to go."

Ava's gaze captured his. "You told her you couldn't, didn't you?" When he hesitated, her eyes widened. "You didn't."

He nodded. "I told her I'd go." Sean reached for her hand. "She looked at me with those blue eyes, and I couldn't say no."

Ava pressed her hands to her cheeks. "This can't be good."

"Do you want me to go in there and tell her I can't make it?" He started for Mica's bedroom. "I will. It'll break her heart, but I understand what you're trying to do."

Ava grabbed his arm bringing him to a halt. "No. You're right. It'll break her heart." She let go of him and drew in a deep breath. "I should have seen this coming. She's been curious about her friends' fathers. She sees them come to get their children at her school. I guess she's feeling the loss." Ava's eyes filled with tears. She blinked them back and lifted her chin. "I'm sorry. You got a lot more than you bargained for when you agreed to go out with me."

"I did," he said and brushed away a tear that found its way down her cheek. "So far, I have no regrets."

He chucked her beneath the chin. "No reneging on cooking dinner for me. It's been a long time since I've had a homecooked meal."

Ava nodded. "You're on."

"And if it's all right with you, I'll be at Mica's school on Monday, as promised, for Daddy Day. We can untangle it afterward."

Ava cupped his cheek, leaned up and brushed her lips across his. "Thank you."

Sean caught her around the waist and crushed her to him, claiming her lips in a kiss like their first...hot, deep and not nearly long enough.

He tore himself away and exited. "Lock the door behind me," he said.

Ava nodded and closed the door.

Sean waited until he heard the click of the deadbolt engaging before he climbed into his truck and drove away.

He looked in his rearview mirror at the little cottage with two beautiful blondes tucked safely inside.

All he could think was how much he'd wanted to stay.

CHAPTER 5

"WE SHOULD BE AT THE OFFICE," Ava said as she climbed out of Leslie's car and hurried toward Mica's school. "I didn't mean for you to take off as well. I felt like I needed to be there for when Sean leaves and Mica realizes he's not coming back."

Leslie stopped her at the front door of the school. "How do you know he's not coming back?"

"Because I told him I didn't want to confuse Mica by introducing men into her life."

"But didn't that already happen?" Leslie cocked an eyebrow.

"Not intentionally. I should have been more careful. Next time, I'll drive and leave my date at the restaurant."

Leslie shook her head. "Honey, that's not how dates work. Kissing in public isn't the same as kissing in private."

Ava's cheeks heated. "Who said we kissed?"

Leslie laughed and pointed a finger toward Ava. "Ha! You did kiss. I knew it."

Ava frowned at her friend and boss. "That's playing dirty."

"It worked, didn't it." Leslie tipped her head toward the school. "It's five minutes after ten o'clock. If he showed up, he'll be in there with Mica now. What if he's good with her? Do you really want to keep her from seeing him again?"

Ava sighed. "Sean and I went into this dating thing with the same goals in mind. We don't want a lasting relationship. We just wanted to go out a few times and that's it."

"But you liked him, didn't you?"

Again, her cheeks heated. "He's a nice guy."

"And he kisses good, huh?" Leslie's lips curled into a wicked smile. "And you're telling me that after a couple of dates, you won't want to see him again? And you won't miss kissing him?"

She shrugged. "I don't want to get involved. It wouldn't be fair to Mica."

Leslie's smile sank. "What about being fair to Ava? You deserve to be happy."

Ava forced a smile to her lips. "I'm happy. I have a great life. I have a beautiful little girl and a home I'm paying for with money I earn. What more could I ask for?"

"An adult to share it with. Someone to bump up against at night," Leslie listed. "Sex?"

"Sex is overrated."

"Says a woman who hasn't had it in too many years to count."

"It's only been six years," Ava said. "And I have—"

"—a BOB." Leslie held up her hand. "Does BOB kiss like Sean?" She crossed her arms over her chest.

Ava's lips twisted. "No." Sean had made her vibrator obsolete. In fact, Ava had put BOB in a box in the top of her closet. She'd almost thrown him away. He wasn't human, he didn't make her feel the way Sean had made her feel on their one and only date. Leslie had been correct when she'd more or less made it clear that BOB wasn't a replacement for real, flesh-and-blood male interaction.

Now that she'd been kissed, Ava was afraid there was no going back. She wanted to see Sean again. And she wanted him to kiss her like he had that night.

"He got under your skin," Leslie said. It wasn't a question. She could see it as plain as if Ava had told her the fact.

Sean had gotten under Ava's skin. And she wanted so much more.

The whole situation was a mess. Now that she wanted more, she'd already laid the groundwork for less, insisting to Sean and BODS that she didn't want a long-term relationship, when in fact, she could imagine such a relationship with a man like Sean.

Damn. She was in way over her head.

"Come on," Leslie said. "You're overthinking this. Let's go spy on your lover."

"He's not my lover," Ava muttered.

"Yet," Leslie said and stepped out with the confidence of someone who knew she was right.

How did the woman know? Sean might decide to run the other direction once he'd sat in a room full of kindergarten kids.

They entered the school and went directly to the office to sign in.

"Glad you called ahead to allow Sean in for Daddy Day," the school secretary said, her smile too bright. "He's so dreamy."

"Sean?"

The secretary blinked and pulled herself together. "He insisted we call him by his first name. What a sweet man. And Mica was so excited when we called her to the office to escort him back to her room."

"Thank you. Is it possible to sneak a peek at the class?" Ava asked.

"Certainly." The secretary made out name tags for them. "They should be having cupcakes and punch right now. Go on back."

Ave led the way out of the office and down the long hallway.

"Did you find out why Sean doesn't want a lasting relationship?" Leslie asked.

Ava's brow dipped. "He didn't say, but he did tell me that his father wasn't very loving, and he thought there was a lot to genetics."

"Is that it?" Leslie shot a glance toward Ava. "He's afraid he'll be like his father?"

"I think so." Ava's heart hurt for the young Sean. Children needed to know they were loved.

"Tag said he met Sean's father once, at Sean's brother's funeral. Said he was a real son of a bitch." Leslie clapped her hand over her mouth and looked around.

Thankfully, there weren't any small children roaming the hallways to hear Leslie's curse.

"Sean lost a brother?" Ava asked.

"From what Tag said, Sean's brother committed suicide after leaving active duty."

Ava's belly knotted. What a horrible end to a young man's life. No wonder Sean didn't want to commit to relationships. With a jerk for a father and a brother who'd ended his own life, where did that leave Sean?

Ava had the sudden urge to hug the man and hold him until all the pain went away. That wasn't realistic. Nor would Sean want her pity. He was a proud man.

"Here we are," Ava whispered, as they came to a halt a few steps short of the open door of Mica's classroom.

The sound of children laughing and talking came from inside, along with the deeper voices of their daddies.

Ava's heart swelled and pinched at the same time.

"I shouldn't spy," Ava said.

"You can't get cold feet now," Leslie muttered.

"I shouldn't spy, but I'm going to anyway." She leaned around the corner and peered into the room.

The children were all seated at little tables. Grown men sat on the floor at the tables with their kindergarten students.

Ava picked out Sean, seated at a table in the far corner. Mica sat beside him, drinking punch and smiling so brightly it hurt Ava to watch. She was so happy to have a man show up to Daddy Day.

"Well? What's happening?" Leslie asked, leaning around Ava to look inside. "Oh, look. Are they all so sweet?" She grinned. "Does a body good to see so many men take an interest in their children's lives."

Ava agreed.

Seeing Mica so happy made her reconsider her stance on not bringing another man into her daughter's life. Even Sean had said that not all men were assholes. Some were very good at accepting children as their own, even if they weren't of their own blood.

She watched in silence as Sean sat patiently eating cupcakes and drinking punch with Mica. Ava could hear the murmur of Mica's voice as she talked nonstop.

The man had to be bored out of his mind. But he didn't show it. He smiled and nodded as if soaking in every word coming out of the child's mouth.

Ava loved Mica and knew her daughter well. The girl could talk until she was blue in the face. Sometimes, Ava wondered if she ever took a breath.

"Wow, he's so patient with her," Leslie noted.

"Yes, he is," Ava agreed. He was definitely the kind of man a girl could easily fall in love with. What woman could resist a man who rescued kittens and indulged a little girl's fantasy of having a daddy show up to her school function?

The teacher clapped her hands to get the attention of the children, then asked them to collect all of the trash and bring it to the trash can at the front of the class.

The fathers stood, preparing to leave.

Mica's smile faded as she stared up at Sean.

He winked at her and bent to give her a big hug.

Mica flung her arms around his neck and hugged hard.

Ava's throat constricted, and she pressed a hand to her chest. How had she not seen how much Mica wanted a father in her life?

She'd done everything to be both to her daughter, but she wasn't a father figure and she couldn't marry a man just to give Mica a father. This one thing she couldn't do for her daughter, and it made her feel like a failure. She knew the feeling was ridiculous, yet she still felt it.

Sean hugged Mica one more time, nodded to the teacher and thanked her for being a good hostess.

Mica's young teacher blushed and smiled back at Sean. "Please, come back to visit our class. We'd love to hear all about your life as a Navy SEAL."

Ava's hands curled into fists.

Was Mica's teacher flirting with Sean?

The teacher flipped her hair back over her shoulder, smiled and batted her eyes.

"Did you see that?" Leslie whispered. "Mica's teacher is coming on to Sean. Oops, we'd better get out of here before we're caught. The men are headed out." Leslie stepped back from the doorway.

Ava stood a moment longer, unable to pull her gaze from Sean.

When he turned toward the door, Ava jerked back out of view.

"He's coming, isn't he?" Leslie said.

"Yes. Come on." Ava turned and half-walked and half-ran down the long hallway, sure Sean would see her before she reached the end. And how embarrassing would it be if he caught her spying on him? Too embarrassing!

Leslie eventually caught up with her, breathing hard. "What the hell?"

"I didn't want him to catch us staring."

"So, we're breaking all the rules they make the kids follow by running down the hall?" Leslie chuckled in between breathing. "You're a case. You know that?"

Ava rounded the corner before she slowed to a walk. "Yes, I'm beginning to think I am." She turned to Leslie. "I thought I knew what I wanted. Now...I don't know."

"I tell you...when you find the one, it changes your world," Leslie said. Her gaze shifted to the window overlooking the playground. "No one else seems quite right."

"How do you know?" Ava asked. "And what if he doesn't feel the same?"

"Honey, you'll know. Your heart will know. You just have to listen to it." She frowned. "And if he doesn't feel the same, you have to have faith that everything will work out in the long run. Some take longer to figure things out than others."

"MICA, I have to go to work now," Sean said as he released his hug on the little girl and straightened. He'd swear he'd seen Ava at the classroom door a moment ago, but when he'd looked again, she wasn't there. Either that, or he was hallucinating.

The past three nights, he hadn't slept without dreaming about the blonde with the incredibly blue eyes. In those dreams, she'd worn that impossibly miniscule black dress. And each time, she'd been barefoot. He woke up feeling like she'd been there, close enough to hold, to kiss and to make love with.

Which made him believe he'd really been hallucinating. She had a job and couldn't afford to miss work, or she wouldn't have the money to pay the mortgage on her little cottage or hire a plumber to fix the drain.

Sometimes, Sean hated that he made so much money and others didn't. Granted, he donated a lot of funds to suicide prevention and St. Jude's Children's Hospital. He wished he could anonymously donate to Ava and Mica to have their little house fixed up even more. He wondered if it was so old that the wiring was substandard. He worried that it was and would end up burning down.

That led him to worrying about them being inside it if that happened.

When Monday had finally rolled around, Sean was happy to go to Mica's school to see for himself that she was all right. He liked the little girl and didn't want anything bad to happen to her or to her mother.

"When will you come see me again?" Mica asked as she walked him toward the door, her hand in his.

Her question reminded him that Ava didn't want him stringing her along with false expectations.

"I don't know, Mica. I'm very busy. It might be a while."

She beamed up at him. "I understand. I'll be happy whenever you can make it." The child stopped at the door and stared up at him. "Do you like my mama?"

Sean nodded. "Of course, I do."

Mica's grin broadened. "She's the best."

"Yes, she is." He rubbed the top of Mica's head. "She takes good care of you."

"I think she likes you, too," Mica said. "I saw you kissing." She covered her mouth with her hand and giggled.

Sean's lips twitched as he fought to hide a smile. The little girl had been spying on them. "Did that bother you?"

She shook her head. "No. People who love each other kiss."

"You don't understand…" Sean started.

When Mica stared up at him quizzically, she made him rethink what he was about to say. Sean clamped his lips shut and studied the top of Mica's head. "Never mind," he finally said. "I need to go." He'd have to fade out of Mica's life. Being direct with the girl would be too hard. He couldn't stand the thought of making her cry. Or her mother, for that matter.

Sean waved one last time and left the classroom, hurrying down the hallway to the exit. He turned in his visitor's pass and left the school.

Outside in the Texas sunshine, he drew in a deep breath and let it out.

"Hey, handsome, do you come here often?" a familiar voice said behind him.

Sean spun to face Ava with a smile on her face. Automatically, his hands reached for her, pulled her into his arms and sealed her mouth with his.

Her hands circled the back of his neck and pulled him closer, deepening the kiss.

For a moment, they were suspended in time and space, living, breathing and existing in that kiss.

When Sean finally broke away, he pressed his forehead to hers, his breath ragged. "I missed you."

She chuckled. "I missed you, too."

"Were you at Mica's classroom door a few minutes ago?"

Her cheeks flushed a soft pink. "Yes."

He closed his eyes, a smile tilting his lips. "Thank God. I thought I was seeing things." He didn't tell her he'd been dreaming about her. That might make him sound a little unstable and stalkerish.

"You weren't." She leaned back and stared up into his eyes. "Thank you for being there for Mica. I know your being there for Daddy Day made her happier than I've seen her in a long time."

"I kept my promise, but even more than that, I enjoyed it."

"You're kidding, right?" Ava laughed, feeling a little

lightheaded with desire. "You know you don't have to say things you don't mean just to impress me."

"I know." He kissed her again, lightly this time. "I was going to call you today."

"You were?" She looked up into his eyes.

"We didn't set a date and time for our second date."

She smiled. "We didn't. I was waiting until after Daddy Day to make our arrangements."

"Did you think I'd change my mind after Daddy Day?"

"The thought crossed my mind," Ava admitted. "Not many men can take one for the man-team and spend a morning drinking punch and eating cupcakes with a bunch of five-year-olds."

He puffed out his chest. "I'm stronger than I look."

She smiled softly. "You look pretty strong to me. A guy doesn't make it into the Navy SEALs unless he's strong."

"And wily." He winked. "Don't forget wily. And a team player."

She laughed. "Name the date and time, and I'll make up a tuna casserole you won't forget."

"Now, you're pulling my leg."

"I am," she admitted. "Although, I do make a damned good tuna casserole. I was thinking more along the lines of lasagna and garlic toast. Those are comfort foods to me."

"That would be steak and potatoes for me."

"I could do that, but it would break my budget for the rest of the week."

"No, don't do that. I haven't had a good lasagna in forever. I look forward to going Italian with you."

She gave him a quick nod. "When?"

"Want to go for Saturday?"

"I'd love to."

"And be ready to stay out late. I want to take you dancing."

"I haven't been dancing in long time. I'm not sure I remember how." Her heart beat faster at the thought of rubbing bellies on a dance floor with the handsome SEAL. "What should I wear?"

"Jeans and cowboy boots, if you have them." He grinned. "We're going to the Ugly Stick Saloon to kick up our heels."

"The Ugly Stick Saloon?" Ava asked, curious.

"Yup. It's a little out in the boonies, but worth the drive."

"Lasagna and dancing." She grinned. "Not sure the two go together, but if you're willing...you're on."

He laughed and pulled her close, his hands sliding low on her back.

She nodded, her smile slipping, her pulse picking up.

Would he kiss her again? She held her breath, praying he would.

He lowered his head, his lips hovering over hers. "Until Friday."

Ava closed her eyes, her entire body anticipating his lips touching hers.

Then he was gone, leaving her standing there in the parking lot, swaying slightly, her knees no sturdier than Jell-O.

"Psst!" Leslie's voice called out to her softly, cutting through Ava's stupor.

"Ava!" Leslie's call finally pulled Ava back to earth. "Let's go before the school calls the cops on us for loitering."

Ava slipped into the passenger seat of Leslie's car and leaned back in her seat.

Leslie laughed and started the engine, pulling out of the parking lot onto the main road in front of the school. "Girl, you've got it bad. And he played you so well."

Ava frowned and tipped her head toward Leslie. "Played me? What do you mean?"

"The law of scarcity. He had you practically begging to be kissed, and then left you hanging."

Heat flooded Ava's cheeks. "Did I look like I was begging?" She pressed her palms to her face.

"Honey, you were practically standing on your toes to get that kiss he didn't give you." Again, she laughed. "What a charmer. He had you in the palm of his hand. Now, you'll be a basket case until you see him again."

Leslie was absolutely right. Ava's body was hot with desire. And it was only Monday.

"When do you see him again?" Leslie asked.

"Saturday," Ava wailed.

With a smile, Leslie switched lanes and drove toward downtown Austin and her office complex where BODS was located. "We need to make sure you're ready for your next date. I believe we have some shopping in order."

"I don't have a lot of money for a new wardrobe," Ava warned.

"You'd be surprised at what you can find at the resale shops. Where's he taking you this time?"

"I'm going to cook dinner for him and then he's taking me dancing." Ave's brow puckered. "To some place called the Ugly Stick Saloon.

Leslie hooted. "He's taking you to a favorite haunt. That's big. He's never brought a date to the Ugly Stick." Leslie wrinkled her nose. "He's picked up women there, but never brought one from outside. I know Sean and his friends. It's likely they'll all be there. That's big when a man introduces you to his friends."

"He didn't mention any friends."

"No, but I guarantee, they will be there." She shot a grin toward Ava. "I'll make sure."

Ava shook her head. "Don't put him on the spot. He might not want to introduce me to his friends."

"Honey, if he's taking you to the Ugly Stick, he's sharing you with his friends." Leslie stared through the windshield. "These friends of his are as close as blood brothers. He'd do anything for them, and they'd do anything for him. If they like you, it's all good."

Her excitement over meeting Sean's friends waned. "What if they don't like me?"

Leslie touched her arm. "Honey, if they don't like you, it's their own damned fault. You're amazing, and they'll see that."

Leslie's assurances only slightly reassured her.

One thing stood out over all others.

She was having a second date with the handsome Navy SEAL. This time, she'd be careful to make sure Mica wasn't involved.

Now that her daughter had had a man at Daddy Day, she'd be even more insistent to see Sean. That couldn't happen. When Sean left, he'd leave a gaping hole in Mica's heart and life. The exact reason Ava didn't want her to meet or interact with the dates she went on. If she was a really good mother, she'd give up the dates and stay home in the evening with her little girl.

Unfortunately, or fortunately, Leslie had been correct. Ava had needed stimulating, adult male conversation to remind her that she was an individual with needs that didn't involve her small daughter.

Now that she'd unleashed her inner beast, she wasn't sure she could turn it off and sink back into her dull, boring existence. Nor did she want to.

.   .   .

"AVA...YOO-HOO."

Ava glanced up. "Sorry, did you say something?"

Leslie grinned. "Several times. Don't forget, you and Mica are going with me and Emma to the county fair this Friday night, and she's staying the night with Auntie Leslie afterward. So, be sure to hype her up with all the sweets before you let me have her."

"Thanks, Leslie," Ava said. "Mica is looking forward to it." She was blessed to have such good friends from the Get a Grip Grief Group. She wasn't sure how she'd have survived without them.

Now, Friday would pass quickly at the fair, bringing her closer to the next day and her date with Sean. A shiver of excitement rippled through her.

Saturday couldn't get there soon enough.

CHAPTER 6

SEAN SPENT the week taking care of his many business and financial responsibilities. On more than one occasion, he'd gone by Leslie's office building. He'd almost stopped to ask if Ava would like to go for coffee or lunch.

Given that she'd been very specific about not starting a relationship that would last more than a couple of dates, he'd driven by without stopping. He told himself he'd see her Saturday night. That was plenty soon enough.

Then why did the time drag until Friday rolled around? One week after his first date with Ava had seemed like a lifetime.

He was driving past Leslie's office building in downtown Austin again, when his cellphone rang in his truck. Caller ID indicated Frank Cooper Johnson was calling.

Sean pressed the phone button on his steering wheel and pulled to a stop at a traffic light. "Hey, Coop."

"Decker," he said in his usual abrupt manner. "Got plans for the night?"

"I had big plans to call out for pizza and watch reruns of the A&M game here in my Austin pad."

"Not headed out to the ranch?"

"Not tonight. I'll probably go on Sunday and spend the week." He couldn't stand the idea of another week trolling downtown Austin, foolishly hoping to catch a glimpse of Ava coming out of Leslie's office building. "Why? Got anything better going than pizza and reruns?"

"Maybe," Coop said. "The gang is headed to the Travis County Fair. Want to meet us there?"

The thought of being in a crush of people made Sean cringe. Yet the idea of staying in his penthouse apartment...alone...was far worse. "I'm in. What time?"

Coop set the time and the meeting location and rang off.

He wasn't thrilled about being out in the heat or the crowds. However, being with his friends would help pass the time better than lounging on his couch, fast-forwarding through a dismal game the Aggies had lost by one point.

With less than an hour to get to the fairgrounds,

find parking and meet up with his friends, Sean figured he'd better get moving.

He swung by his apartment and changed out of his business suit. Once he was comfortable in jeans, a short-sleeve blue denim shirt and cowboy boots, he hurried back out to his truck and drove to the fair-grounds.

True to his word, Coop was waiting near the funhouse with Gage, Tag and Moose.

When Sean showed up, they headed for the beer tent.

As they were waiting in line for their first round of beer, Sean looked around at the families with small children and thought of Mica. She would love coming to the fair. The raucous music and colorful booths would have her rushing from one event or ride to another.

"Are you still on for the Ugly Stick Saloon tomorrow night?" Gage asked him.

"I am."

"Tag tells us you have a date." Moose turned with the first of the beers and handed it to Sean.

He took it and drank a long swallow of the cool liquid. "Yes, I'll be bringing a date."

Moose passed the next beer down the line of friends.

Tag took his cup and grinned. "He met her through BODS."

Moose handed a beer to Coop and retrieved the

last two, giving one to Gage. "I thought you didn't believe in Leslie's matchmaking system," Moose said.

Sean shrugged. "Tag and Leslie convinced me it wouldn't hurt to give it a try."

"Isn't this your second date with the same woman?" Coop asked.

Sean cringed, hoping they wouldn't continue to grill him on his foray into online dating. "Yes, it will be our second date. And no, I'm not marrying her. She and I aren't interested in long-term relationships. It stops at dating."

"Uh-huh," Moose said and tipped back his cup for a long drink before adding, "That's what we all said. Just a date. Now three of us are engaged. Sorry to inform you, old man, but your single days are numbered."

Sean frowned. "I'm not like the rest of you. I didn't go into BODS to find a wife. I only want a date with someone who isn't after me for my money or for a ring on her finger. BODS found me just that kind of woman. You'll get to meet her tomorrow night." He glared at them. "*If* you promise to act nice around her."

"You mean we can't burp and fart in her presence?" Moose asked.

"Do what you want," Sean said. "I'm bringing her to the Ugly Stick Saloon to get in a little two-stepping."

"She dances?"

"I'll let you know tomorrow night," Sean said.

"Can't wait to meet the woman who has you all wound up like a top." Gage lifted his cup full of beer. "To falling in love."

"To love!" Coop, Tag and Moose said in unison, as they lifted their cups into the air.

Sean frowned. "It's not love. We're only dating. Nothing more."

"He sure is protesting a lot," Coop said.

"And it is his second date with this woman," Moose pointed out. "That has to be a record." He winked.

"Hey…" Tag interrupted their tormenting of Sean to point toward the fairgrounds entrance. "Isn't that Emma, Fiona, Jane and Leslie?"

"Yeah," Coop said. "Who's the blonde with the kid?"

Sean's heartrate jumped up. He spun toward the front gate, his gaze going immediately to the petite blonde in the center of the group of women. Her hand rested on Mica's shoulder. They were laughing and smiling as they walked through the gate.

"That's Ava and Mica," Tag said, elbowing Sean in the ribs. "Ava is Decker's match from BODS."

"You don't say," Gage murmured. "I can see why you haven't said much about her. You don't want anyone else getting a jump on you. Good thing I've found the love of my life." He winked and strode forward to take Fiona into his arms, kissing her soundly.

"Me, too," Coop said and joined Emma, wrapping his arms around her in a fierce hug.

"I like my woman tall enough I can look her in the eye," Moose, an NFL football champ, said and smiled at his lady love, former model Jane "Angel" Gentry. He held out his hand. She took it and let him bring her in for a long, sexy kiss.

"Leslie," Tag held out his hand. Leslie placed hers in his. "I didn't know you ladies would be here tonight."

She frowned. "I told you we would be."

Tag gave her a stern glance and shook his head. "Shh. I didn't tell the others I knew. I'd like to keep it our little secret."

She laughed and swatted at his arm. "You're impossible."

He hugged her and kissed the top of her head. "Good thing you love me."

Sean tried to see around the others to where Ava and Mica stood. When they finally moved to the side, his gaze met Ava's and he smiled. She smiled back.

Mica spotted him, grinned and ran toward him, her arms flung wide. "Daddy!"

"What?" Tag asked.

Sean ignored his buddies as they all turned to see what Mica was talking about.

The little girl wrapped her arms around Sean's neck and held on.

Sean lifted her off the ground and held her close. He'd never felt so loved as he did at that moment. "Hey, Mica, good to see you."

"I missed you," she whispered in his ear. "I prayed you would come to see me and read another book to me. When you didn't, I was afraid I'd made you mad or something."

He leaned back and stared into the pretty little girl's eyes. "No way. It's just that you have your house, and I have mine. I can't be at your house all the time."

"Not even some of the time?"

"Sweetheart, I'm not your daddy," he said. "I'd be one very lucky man if I were. You're pretty amazing."

"But you could be," Mica said. "Layla got a new dad just the other day. She said all her mama had to do was marry him." Mica looked over Sean's shoulder. "Mama, can't you marry Mr. Decker so I can have a daddy, too?"

Ava's eyes rounded, and her face paled. "Oh, baby, it's not that easy."

"Layla said it was," Mica said, her brow dipping. "And now she has a new daddy. I want a daddy. Please."

Sean stared across at Ava, his stomach tightening into a hard knot at the stricken look on her face.

She held out her arms to her daughter. "Oh, baby,

it really isn't that easy. The mommy and the man have to be in love and want to get married."

"Can't you love Mr. Decker?" Mica begged, her big blue eyes filling with tears. "He's very nice, and he doesn't mind sitting on the floor in my classroom."

Sean looked around, noticing that his friends had all deserted him, leaving him and Ava alone to deal with Mica's demands. Before the little girl had a total meltdown, he had to do something. "Mica, let's talk about this later. We're at the county fair. We're supposed to play and have fun."

"Will you play with us?" Mica's bottom lip trembled, tugging at Sean's heart.

He glanced at Ava.

Mica's mother shrugged. "If you don't mind."

"I'd be honored," Sean said.

Mica frowned in confusion.

Sean laughed. "Yes. I'd love to." He tossed her up in the air and caught her.

Mica giggled and clung to him with a fierce hug. "Thank you, Mr. Decker," she said loud enough for her mother to hear. Then she whispered in his ear. "You'll always be Daddy to me."

Warmth spread through Sean. He tried not to let the little girl get to him, but it was too late. She had him wrapped completely around her little finger.

He set her on her feet and held onto one of her hands.

She reached her free hand out to Ava, who took it with a smile.

"What shall we do first?" her mother asked.

"The Ferris wheel!" Mica cried.

Sean and Ava walked to the ride with Mica swinging between them, laughing and talking the entire time.

This was how a family was supposed to be. Not how his father had raised him and his younger brother. There hadn't been fun trips to the fairgrounds or walks in the park holding hands with his father and mother.

His mother had run off when Sean had just turned seven, leaving her sons to be raised by a cranky man who hadn't even liked kids. He'd dealt with the stress of raising two rambunctious boys by drowning himself in alcohol and yelling whenever Sean and his brother Patrick passed by his lounge chair. Sometimes, he'd taken swings at one of them, knocking a kid across the room.

Sean vowed never to have children for fear of turning into a man like his father. No child deserved a parent like that.

With little Mica looking up at him like he'd actually hung the moon, Sean had no choice but to show the girl a good time.

The more she laughed and smiled, the more relaxed and happier Sean was. And the happier Mica was, the more Ava smiled.

It might not have been her idea to share the county fair experience with the man she'd only ever wanted to date, but she was having a good time, if the smile on her face was any indication.

On the Ferris wheel, Mica clung to Sean and Ava's hands and stared out at the fair below with all the colorful lights and sounds. The smell of popcorn and funnel cakes filled the air.

Sean glanced over the top of Mica's head at Ava and smiled. For such a busy man, he couldn't think of anywhere else he'd rather be at that moment. Something felt good and right about sitting on the bench, swinging in the air with two of the prettiest girls he'd ever met.

The moment wouldn't last, but the memory would. He closed his eyes and committed it to that special place in his brain where all the happiest thoughts resided.

When they got off the ride, Mica dragged them to a shooting game where Sean, Mica and Ava tried to shoot water at duck targets.

Though Ava and Mica tried, they couldn't knock the ducks over.

One after the other, Sean knocked over the targets, winning a bright purple unicorn for Mica.

The child was beside herself, she was so happy, nearly hugging the stuffing out of that fat, purple unicorn.

They met up with the others in front of the funhouse.

"Are you going in?" Tag asked. "Leslie and I have been through twice already. We almost got lost in the mirrors."

Leslie laughed and leaned into Tag's arm. "This graceful guy nearly broke his nose on one of the mirrors. I told him it was a mirror, but he didn't believe me. He thought it was reflections bouncing off the walls. So, he walked right into it." She laughed out loud. "Funniest thing I've ever seen."

"We were just about to go in," Coop said, holding Emma's hand.

"I want to go," Mica cried.

"Let me take Mica," Leslie said. "I know the way through now."

"Mica, do you want to go with Auntie Leslie?"

Mica nodded, clutching her purple unicorn under her arm. She reached for Leslie's hand with her free one, and off they went, ducking through the door of the funhouse trailer.

"Are you game?" Sean asked Ava.

She smiled and nodded. "Lead the way."

He held out his hand, and she took it.

For the first time that night, he was touching Ava. That zing of awareness traveled from where their palms connected, all the way up his arm to spread through his chest, warming him all over his body.

They silently waited their turn to enter the

funhouse. When the carnival worker waved them in, Ava glanced up at Sean.

He smiled and circled his arm round the lower part of her back. "Let's do this."

Once inside, they walked through a dark area where spooky clown puppets sprang out, laughing maniacally.

Ava shrank into Sean, wrapping her arm around him to get even closer. The clowns ended in a maze of mirrors.

One after the other, Sean and Ava bumped into walls of mirrors, until they were so turned around Sean didn't know which way was forward and which was backward.

Ava laughed and turned in his arms, planting her hands on his chest. "I think we might be stuck in here for a while."

His hands rose to rest on her hips. "That would be all right with me," he said softly, the sound of clown laughter fading in the intensity of Ava's gaze.

"Me, too."

Then he pulled her closer and pressed his lips to hers in a kiss that felt as if it originated in the depths of his soul.

She wound her fingers into the hair at the back of his head and dragged him even closer, pressing her breasts to his chest, her hips to his.

Sean wished the moment could have lasted forever.

A shout of laughter sounded from somewhere in the maze of mirrors as another couple left the clowns behind and started into the maze.

"We have to go," he said, regret weighing on his words.

"What if I don't want to?" she asked.

"Then the carnies will come in and boot our asses out." He brushed his lips across hers in the briefest of kisses. "Come on." He pulled her hand through the crook of his elbow and guided her through the rest of the maze and out into the night.

Ava frowned. "You knew how to get out all along?"

"Not at first. But then I was having so much fun, I didn't want it to end." He smiled as he led her down the steps to the ground where Leslie and Mica waited.

"We found our way through. Auntie Leslie knew the way," Mica said. She stood beside Leslie, leaning against the woman. Then she yawned and rubbed her eyes.

"Someone is getting sleepy," Leslie said.

"I'm not tired." Mica yawned again.

"Sure, you're not tired." Ava's gaze met Leslie's. "Do you want me to take her home?"

Leslie shook her head. "No way. Mica and I have a date with some chocolate milk and cookies. Then we're going to stay up late and watch cartoons until midnight."

Ava snorted. "You're a bad influence for my child."

"It won't hurt for her to stay up late every once in a while." Leslie leaned toward Ava. "Besides, I don't think someone will make it past the milk and cookies."

"I'm not sleepy," Mica insisted.

"That's right. We have a plan for the night, and sleeping isn't part of it." Leslie winked at Ava. "Don't worry. We'll have so much fun, Mica will want to move in with Auntie Leslie for good."

Mica shook her head, her gaze going to Ava and then Sean. "I can't leave my mama forever." She tugged on Leslie's hand until the woman bent close enough for Mica to whisper in her ear. "I might have a daddy soon, if Mama falls in love with Mr. Decker."

Though she'd whispered, those close enough could hear her every word.

Ava blushed, and Sean clenched his fists. Mica's mother would be worried they were setting her up for a fall. When the dating ended, the little girl would be disappointed to know she wasn't getting the daddy she wanted so badly.

The thought made Sean sad for Mica. Unfortunately, things didn't always turn out the way you wanted. The sooner she learned that, the better off she'd be.

"I'll stay one night with Auntie Leslie," Mica said. "But then I'm going home."

"Fair enough. One night." Leslie looked around at

the other women who'd arrived with her. "I'll see you all tomorrow night?"

Jane, Emma and Fiona nodded.

"We have some boot-scootin' to do," Emma said. She leaned into Coop. "I've been teaching Coop how to two-step. I think he's ready to show you all what he's learned." She smiled up at the man.

Coop grimaced. "I've learned I'm all left feet, and this angel has sacrificed a couple of her toes to the cause. I'll be out there, but it might not be pretty." He hugged Emma close.

"Don't let him fool you. He's doing amazing." She leaned up on her toes to press her lips to his.

"On that note, Mica and I are headed out," Leslie said. "Sean, do you mind giving Ava a ride home?"

Sean nodded. "My pleasure."

Ava frowned. "Are you sure? I could catch a cab."

"I'm sure." Sean gave Leslie a chin lift. "I'll get her home."

Emma bent to give Mica a hug. "Sleep tight, little bug."

"I will," Mica promised. She held up her arms to Ava. "Sleep tight, Mama."

Ava hugged her tightly and kissed her cheek. "I'll see you in the morning."

"I'll bring her by around ten," Leslie said. "After we've had waffles and strawberries."

"Waffles and strawberries? Yum!" Mica skipped alongside Leslie as they headed for the exit.

"I'll make sure they get home safely," Tag said and left the group.

"We're calling it a night as well," Coop said, smiling down at Emma. "We must be getting old."

Emma slapped his chest playfully. "Speak for yourself, old man." She took his hand. "See you all tomorrow night."

"We're riding with them," Gage said. He and Fiona followed Emma and Coop to the car park.

"I'd like to say that leaves the four of us, but Jane and I have a charity event at the children's hospital in the morning. We need to get some sleep so that we can get up early." They exited, leaving Ava and Sean standing in front of the funhouse, alone.

"You really don't have to give me a ride home. I can get there on my own," Ava said.

"Stop," Sean said. "The BODS deal was that if we didn't want to do something, we didn't have to." He brushed a strand of her hair back from her face. "I want to take you home. Just not yet. Unless you're tired and ready to go." He held his breath and waited for her response.

"I'm not too tired. And I get to sleep in tomorrow." She smiled. "What do you have in mind? Dancing?"

He shook his head. "Nothing so strenuous. You worked all day, and I just want to relax."

"Do you want to get a drink somewhere?"

He nodded. "I do. But I don't want to share you

with a room full of strangers."

Ava's brow puckered. "That's sweet. I think. Where did you have in mind?"

"I have a place here in Austin. I want to show you the view. It's amazing."

Her eyes narrowed, and color suffused her cheeks. "Is that your way of getting me alone to make your move? It's been a long time since I've been with a man, but I watch TV."

He held up his hand. "I promise not to make a move, unless you want me to." He dropped his hand. "Leslie vets all her clients. She runs background checks on them to make sure we don't have a criminal record. I don't force women to sleep with me." His lips twisted. "They usually come willingly. But that's not the point." He held out his hand. "Trust me. The view is amazing." He held out his hand. "Or I can take you straight home, and you won't have to worry about this man making his move. It's your choice."

Ava hesitated a moment longer. "I haven't known you long, but I feel in my bones that I can trust you." She laid her hand in his. "Show me this amazing view."

Sean's chest tightened as he pulled her hand through the crook of his arm and led her to his truck. He told himself that all he wanted was the pleasure of her company.

Well, it wasn't all he wanted. But it would have to be enough for now.

CHAPTER 7

Ava stepped into the elevator of one of the high-rise buildings in downtown Austin.

Sean had gotten them past the security guard at the entrance, and now he used a key card to access the penthouse suite at the top of the structure.

Ava hadn't really thought more about the fact that he'd taken her to one of the most expensive restaurants in Austin. However, any man who could afford a place at the top of one of the classiest buildings in all of Texas had to have money.

She wasn't sure how she felt about Sean being rich. He didn't act snooty. Nor had he lorded over the wait staff at the expensive restaurant. Sean seemed positively normal.

Then how the heck had he afforded to own the penthouse of this swanky downtown building?

The long ride up the elevator to the top of the

building left her entirely too much time to dwell on the fact she was way out of her depth when it came to Sean Decker. He was an enigma.

And her daughter was quickly falling in love with him as a father figure. She'd have to reiterate her stance on bringing men into Mica's life. Already, the child had unrealistic expectations based on having only met Sean three times.

Had they really only had three encounters with the charismatic Texan? Ava felt like they'd known each other much longer. At the same time, she didn't know much about him, other than what his profile had listed as his preferences and lifestyle.

"How long have you had this apartment?"

Sean shrugged. "Three, maybe four years," he answered. "I live here when I'm working in Austin. I prefer to live out at the ranch. I like to see the stars as well."

She smiled as the door to the elevator opened into the apartment. No hallway, no door to unlock. One minute they were traveling upward on an elevator, the next minute, they were stepping into an apartment bigger than five of her houses all put together.

Ava almost hated to walk across the shiny white and gray marble tiles in her tennis shoes. The rubber soles seemed to be a kind of sacrilege to the classy flooring.

As soon as the elevator closed behind them, Sean hooked her arm and led her over the window. "I really did bring you to my place to see the view. It's not the stars you see in the countryside, but it's beautiful and you can see the twinkle of all the lights shining up from the city."

Ava's breath caught in her throat as she stared down at the beautiful lights of Austin. She could see for miles in most directions through the long line of windows stretched across the length of the penthouse.

"Does it get hot up here during the day with all these windows?" she asked.

"I keep the AC set pretty low. And if that isn't enough, we can take the thermostat even lower. And the shades can be controlled via the room remote control panel." He smiled at Ava. "Can I get you a drink?"

He turned toward the kitchen, set into an alcove at one end of the apartment. "I can offer you anything but a frozen drink."

"Do you have red wine?" Ava asked, suddenly needing something to steady her nerves and give her strength to be around a man who made her knees wobble and butterflies take flight in her belly.

"I do." He pulled a crystal goblet out of a cabinet and a bottle of wine from a rack built into the wall. With the ease of one who'd done it often, Sean opened the bottle of wine and poured half a glass.

He handed the glass to her and crossed to a crystal decanter filled with amber liquid.

"Whisky?" Ava asked.

"Scotch," he said. "I found this brand on a trip to Scotland. The same family had made it for over three hundred years."

Ava sipped the wine, letting the alcohol give her that little bit of buzz that took the edge off her nerves.

While Sean poured his scotch whisky, Ava walked to the windows overlooking Austin. Standing a couple feet away from the glass, she took in the Austin city lights, laid out before her like a blanket of rhinestones. Or in Sean's case, diamonds.

"You didn't tell me you were rich," she said.

"I didn't think it was important to note in the questionnaire," he said. "Does it make a difference?"

Ava's instinct was to say yes. But she couldn't begin to explain why it made a difference. "It shouldn't," she said, instead.

"Shouldn't?" He came to stand beside her in front of the window, carrying his tumbler of scotch. "But it does?"

Ava nodded, looking at Sean's reflection instead of the city lights. Though he wore jeans, a button-down denim shirt and cowboy boots incongruous to the opulence of the penthouse, he looked like he belonged.

Ava stood a foot shorter in her jeans, soft-soled tennis shoes and powder blue sweater, with her hair pulled up in a messy bun at the back of her head. She looked like what she was, a combination of grit, secondhand clothes and bargain store shoes.

She sighed and waved her hand at the beautiful room. "I don't belong here."

Sean frowned. "Do you want to go somewhere else? I only wanted to show you the view."

"It's a beautiful view, but I can't stay." She carried her glass to the massive chef's kitchen with its shiny new appliances and brilliant white countertops that probably cost more than her entire house. She carefully set the wine glass in the sink, having only taken a sip. "Please, could you take me home?"

Sean set the tumbler on an end table and crossed to where she stood in the kitchen. "What's wrong? Why the sudden desire to leave?"

"Leslie's system has some obvious flaws. I didn't ask for any of this in my preferences. I'm a simple girl with peanut butter and jelly tastes. I don't know how to behave in a place like this. I didn't know how to act in the restaurant the other day. This isn't who I am, and I don't know why you've brought me here, what your intention is and how I can extricate myself from the situation." She twisted her hands together.

He took her hands in his. "I'm sorry. I didn't intend to make you uncomfortable." Bringing her fingers to his lips, he pressed a kiss to the backs of the knuckles on her left hand.

Why did his lips have to feel so good against her

skin? "I'm not so uncomfortable as much as I don't feel like I fit in here."

He nodded. "I feel the same. This place has never been me. I don't like how sterile and white it is. Problem is...I'm no decorator. It was easier to leave it as is than to change it." He smiled down at her and brushed his thumb across her cheek.

Her breath caught and held at his touch. "I get that," she said, her voice soft, barely discernable.

"I bought this place because I loved the view. It's not the ranch with all the stars lighting the night, but it has its own beauty." He pulled her into his arms. "If you don't like it here, I can take you home."

Her common sense warred with desire. With Sean standing so close, her logic went on strike, and she couldn't think straight. "No," she found herself saying. "We don't have to leave just yet."

He touched his forehead to hers. "I'm glad, because I didn't want the night to end so soon."

All she had to do was lift her chin a little and she could claim his lips in a soul-defining kiss. Did she dare?

So strong was her desire for this man, she couldn't control her own reactions to him. As if of its own accord, her chin lifted, and she swept her lips across his in a feather-soft kiss.

When she started to pull away, his arms tightened around her, drawing her closer.

"I drove by Leslie's office every day this week."

She frowned. "Why didn't you stop?"

One corner of his mouth quirked. "I didn't want to appear to be a stalker."

"And you think telling me about it will make it any less creepy?" She chuckled at his look of horror. "Don't worry. I thought about you a lot, as well."

Sean pressed a kiss to her forehead. "Is it crazy to want to be with someone that much?"

Ava shrugged. "It must be."

"I know how BODS worked for my friends Coop, Gage and Moose. But they were actively looking for women to spend the rest of their lives with." He bent and kissed the tip of Ava's nose. "You and I had constraints built into our profiles."

"No permanent relationships. Dating only," she said, her voice fading at the end.

Sean rested his forehead against hers. "I'm not certain how this is all supposed to work or how far you want to go with us. It seems a shame that we won't always have a tomorrow."

She raised a finger to press against his lips. "You're thinking too hard," she whispered, raising her face to his, offering her mouth to him, hoping he would accept.

He took her, crushing her lips beneath his, pushing his tongue past her teeth to stroke the length of hers in a tantalizing claim.

Ava leaned into him, her knees no longer capable of supporting her. She wound her hands into the fabric of his shirt and tugged on it until it slipped free of the waistband of his jeans.

Her fingers slipped beneath the denim to touch his naked skin.

He was warm, the muscles of his abdomen taut and firm.

When his hands found the hem of her sweater, she didn't resist. Instead, she pulled her shirt over her head and tossed it to the floor.

Standing in front of him in her jeans and bra, she remembered where they were. The windows of the penthouse overlooked all of the city of Austin. Could all of Austin look into windows?

"Come with me." Sean took her hand and led her past a sofa. He snagged a remote control device and hit a button as he walked. Shades lowered over the big picture windows, blocking out the magical city lights.

Sean didn't stop in the living room. He continued to the opposite end of the huge penthouse, pausing in front of a door that led into a spacious bedroom.

In the center of one wall stood a massive king-size bed covered in a soft white, down comforter.

He stepped inside, still holding Ava's hand, without pulling or tugging. He waited for Ava to make the decision to enter the room.

Her heart pounding against her ribs, she followed him through the door, all the way into the master bedroom.

Sean stopped beside the bed, released her hand and turned to grip her arms in a light grasp she could easily break. "Just say no, and I'll take you out of here and back to your place."

Ava shook her head. Since their first kiss, Ava's dreams had been filled with Sean. "I want to stay."

Raising her hands, she unhooked one button at a time on his denim shirt. She didn't stop until she had all of them loose. Then she pushed the shirt over his broad shoulders and let it fell free to the ground.

Ava drank in the curves and plains of his muscles. She ran her fingers across them, feeling the hardness and strength beneath his smooth skin. She paused at each scar, tracing the jagged lines. "Did they hurt?"

He shrugged. "At the time, all I could think about was getting my team out alive. Pain wasn't an option." Sean captured her hand in his and brought it to his lips. "I want you."

She nodded, knowing this might be their one and only time together. Their deal was clear. No relationship. Tomorrows weren't guaranteed or wanted.

When she'd signed up for this gig, Ava had thought that was what she wanted. Now...she was torn. The thought that this might be their one and only time together made the act even more poignant.

"I haven't done this in a very long time," she whispered.

He pulled her against him and pressed a kiss to her temple. "We can take it slow."

Ava shook her head, the blood humming through her veins, her nerves shooting electrical impulses throughout her body and her core heating. "No. Don't. It's like I'm on fire." She stepped back, reached for the button on her jeans and pushed it through the hole. Before she could grab the tab on her zipper, Sean's hands brushed hers aside.

Slowly, to the point of excruciating pain, he dragged the zipper down, his other hand following the path, slipping into her jeans and her lacy panties to cup her sex.

Ava moaned and pressed into his palm. She grabbed the waistband of her jeans and shoved them down her thighs.

Sean chuckled. "In a hurry?"

"Yes!"

"Let me," he urged, removing his hand from her sex to ease the jeans the rest of the way down her legs.

He followed with kisses and flicks of his tongue down her thighs to the inside bend of her knees, and then lower to the firm curve of her calf.

When he reached her ankles, he pushed the shoe from the back of her heel and slid it from her foot, tossing it to the side.

Once he had both shoes off, Ava stepped free of the jeans.

While he still knelt in front of her, Sean slipped off her socks. Then he kissed his way up her calves and thighs, stopping when he reached the scrap of lace covering her sex.

He looked up at her, his gaze capturing hers.

She nodded, her breath hitching in her throat.

Sean hooked his fingers into the elastic waistband of her panties and slid them over her hips and down her thighs, his knuckles skimming her skin, blazing fire across her nerves.

By the time she stepped free of the panties, Ava's breaths were coming in ragged gasps. She unhooked her bra, letting the straps slide down her arms.

A shiver shook her from head to toe, and her nipples puckered. She hadn't been naked in front of a man since she'd given birth to Mica. Would he notice the stretch marks? Would he find them repulsive?

She waited, her eyes wide, her pulse pounding so loudly against her eardrums she couldn't hear herself think.

Sean's gaze slid over her like a caress. He reached out to cup her face in his palm, brushing his thumb across her cheekbone. "You're beautiful."

She snorted, nervously. "I don't know about that, but I know you're overdressed."

He smiled. "That can be remedied." In seconds, he shed his boots and jeans and stood before her naked, strong and proud.

His cock jutted forward, hard, thick and long.

Ava couldn't help staring at his magnificence, her

mouth suddenly dry. She ran her tongue along her lips, anxious to get started.

"Do I scare you?" He reached for her and pulled her close. "You can change your mind at any time. Just say the word."

"You're kidding, right?" she said, her voice breathless.

"Not at all." He brushed a strand of her hair back behind her ear. "You have to want this as much as I do."

"Oh, dear sweet heaven, I want this." She cupped his face between her hands and leaned up on her toes to press a kiss to his lips. "I want you. Now. Make love to me. Please." She didn't care that she sounded desperate. She wanted this man, his touch, his body.

Sean chuckled, scooped her up in his arms and laid her out on the huge bed. For a moment, he stared down at her, his gaze making her nipples pucker. He reached out and trailed his fingers across her ankle, gripped it and moved it to the side.

He climbed onto the bed, planted his hands on either side of her head and settled his body between her legs. His cock nudged her entrance.

Ava sucked in a breath and held it in anticipation of having all of him inside.

Sean was in no hurry to consummate their evening. He pressed a kiss to her temple, to her forehead and each of her eyelids.

Ava ran her hands over his chest, memorizing

how he felt, how he smelled, how warm he was to the touch.

When he covered her mouth with his, she opened to him, taking his tongue and meeting it with thrusts of her own.

Hunger built at her core and spread throughout her body.

When he'd drunk his fill of her mouth, he spread kisses across her chin and down the long length of her neck. When he reached her breast, he tongued the tip until it hardened into a little bead. Then he sucked it into his mouth and rolled it between his teeth.

Ava arched off the bed, pressing her breast deeper into Sean's mouth.

He sucked on it then moved to the other breast and gave it equal attention until Ava moaned and writhed beneath him. She wanted more. So much more. And soon.

Sean worked his way down her body, trailing kisses and nibbles along each rib. He dipped into her belly button and moved lower to the mound of curls over her sex.

Already fevered and needy, she spread her legs wider and waited for what would come next.

Sean cupped her with his palm and slid a finger into her slick channel, swirling it around. Wet with her juices, he parted her folds and stroked her clit until she lay flat on her back, her head tossing side to side.

Could it get any better than this? She might come apart if it did.

Positioning his head between her legs, he lifted them and draped them over his shoulders. With his tongue, he flicked and licked her clit until Ava forgot how to breathe.

The tingling began where his tongue touched her and spread like lightning throughout her body to the very tips of her fingers and toes.

Ava threaded her hands into his hair and held him there, her body convulsing with her release. Pulsing and shuddering with the waves of sensations washing over her.

He climbed up her body, leaned over and reached into the nightstand to retrieve a little foil packet.

Ava thanked the heavens that Sean had the good sense to think of protection. She certainly wasn't in any way capable of thinking past what was happening below her waist.

All she knew was she'd waited a long time for this, and it was more than she could remember. But now that Pandora's box had been opened, how would she ever be able to walk away from it? From him? From Sean?

SEAN SLIPPED the condom over himself and settled

between Ava's legs. He was so hard and thick, he was afraid he'd hurt her if he moved inside her too fast.

With every ounce of control he could muster, he eased into her, a little at time, giving her body the opportunity to adjust to his size. He wanted their first coupling to be perfect and pain free.

"Can't wait." Ava reached out, grabbed his buttocks and brought him home.

With her channel wrapped tightly around him, he remained deep inside her for a long moment. Then he drew himself almost all the way out and slipped back inside.

She was wet, so very slick and warm.

Sean groaned and pulled back out, settling into a natural, sexy rhythm.

Ava planted her heels on the mattress and met each of his thrusts with ones of her own. The faster he moved, the better it felt until he was pumping in and out of her.

She rested her hands on his hips, digging her fingernails into each cheek.

As the sensations intensified, he held on for as long as he could before he shot over the edge and rocketed into the stratosphere.

One last thrust left him buried deep inside of her, his cock throbbing, his body on fire, a flame he never wanted to put out.

When he finally dropped back to earth, he

collapsed on top of her and rolled them both onto their sides, maintaining their intimate connection.

She cupped his face with her hand and smiled into his eyes. "Wow."

Sean chuckled. "Wow, yourself."

"Is it always this good with you?" she asked.

"I don't know how good it was for you, but it was amazing for me," he said.

"Mmm. It was amazing," Ava said and kissed his chin, his lips and then thrust her tongue between his teeth to caress his.

When she gave him a chance to breathe again, he helped her out of the bed, walking her to the adjoining bathroom where they shared a warm shower and made love again. Thankfully, he had a stash of condoms in the bathroom.

By the time they returned to the bed, he was tired, and she was yawning. He laid down beside her, gathered her into his arms and inhaled the fresh, clean scent of the woman.

Ava laid her cheek against his chest, draped an arm over his hip and sighed.

Sean held her in his arms until her breathing grew deeper and her soft, warm body relaxed completely.

For a long moment he remained awake, absorbing all that had happened and all he was feeling. One thought stood out above all.

He didn't want this to end.

CHAPTER 8

WHEN AVA WOKE, it was dark in the room. At first, she didn't know where she was. Then the weight of an arm over her waist brought back memories of all that had occurred the night before.

She'd made love with Sean, not once, but twice. And she wanted to do it again.

She lay with one leg draped over his thigh and a hand resting on his muscular chest.

Her purely physical reaction to the man was at once exciting and unnerving. Her desire was so strong, it was like an addiction. She couldn't get enough of him and wanted him more than she wanted to breathe.

A desire so strong couldn't be healthy. What would happen when their time together ended, as it surely would? He'd be out of her life, and she'd be alone again.

Just the way she'd wanted it.

In the beginning.

Her reason for keeping her dating life separate from her home life had been to protect Mica from the yoyo of parading multiple men through her world. That reason hadn't changed. Unfortunately, Mica had met this man and wanted him to be the daddy she'd never had.

The more she saw him, the more she'd push the issue until the day came that Sean exercised his right to step out of the picture and never date Ava again.

He'd been just as adamant as she had been about only dating. No long-term relationships.

Ava had to end this before Mica got too entrenched in her feelings for Sean and was hurt when he disappeared out of her life.

Ava eased her hand from Sean's chest and untangled her leg from his. Moving his arm from her waist was a little trickier.

She ended up slipping out from under it and rolling off the bed to land on her hands and knees on the cool, tile floor.

Sean rolled over onto his side.

Ava held her breath, expecting him to wake and ask her where she was going.

When he didn't, she breathed a sigh of relief and went on a hunt to find her clothing with the only light coming from a nightlight glowing from the bathroom.

She found everything but her panties.

Closing the door to the bedroom, she dressed quickly, grabbed her purse and shoes and hurried to the elevator door.

She waited several long moments for the car to arrive, glancing back at the door to the master bedroom, expecting Sean to appear in the doorway at any moment. When the elevator door finally opened, she stepped aboard and let go of the breath she'd been holding.

On the way down, she called a cab. It was waiting for her as she walked past the security desk and out of the building into the night.

Ava made it home without any trouble and let herself into her little house before her emotions caught up with her.

She locked the door, dropped her purse on the floor and ran for her bedroom, kicking off her shoes as she went.

Flinging herself onto the bed, she pulled a pillow up to her chest and let go of the flood of tears that came from where, she didn't know.

What was wrong with her?

Sean was just a man who'd taken her out on a date and just happened to run into her at the county fair. It wasn't as if they had been together since high school. They hadn't started out as best friends. They'd begun as strangers. And then they were in bed and making love like there would be no tomorrow.

Which was the problem. With the way they'd gone into the BODS database, they weren't meant to last. They were supposed to date only and then move on whenever the mood took them.

The big flaw in that premise was that Ava was forming attachments to Sean. And worse...so was Mica.

Which could only end in heartache. Ava cried for Mica. She cried for herself, and she cried for knowing, now, what she'd been missing in her life.

Eventually, Ava cried herself to sleep.

When she woke, she had a splitting headache, her eyes were red-rimmed and puffy, and it was ten o'clock.

Her doorbell rang, forcing her to get out of bed and pad barefooted to open the door.

Mica rushed in, carrying the backpack she'd taken with her to Auntie Leslie's. Her daughter slammed into her legs, hugged her hard and then ran past her into her bedroom. "Love you, Mama!"

Ava pinched the bridge of her nose and moaned. "Love you, too, baby."

"You look like hell," Leslie said.

"Thanks. Nice to see you, too." Ava turned, walked into the kitchen and plugged in the coffee maker.

"You better let me do that," Leslie said, shooing her away from the coffee grinds. "What happened to you?"

Ava collapsed into the seat at the breakfast table

and buried her face in her hands. "I slept in." She glanced up with a grimace.

"Uh huh." Leslie gave her a side-eye glance. "Then how do you explain the tear tracks on your cheeks?"

Ava rubbed her face with her fingertips.

Leslie shook her head as she poured a scoop of coffee into a filter and turned on the machine. "Did Sean make you cry?"

"I don't cry," Ava said.

"And my name isn't Leslie." Her friend pulled out the chair beside her and sat. "What's wrong? And don't tell me nothing, because it's as plain as the smeared mascara on your face."

Ava sat up straighter, ready to tell Leslie to mind her own business.

One look at the concern in her friend's eyes pulled the wind out of Ava's sails and sent her into another useless bout of tears. "I don't know what's wrong with me." Again, she buried her face in her hands and let the tears fall, careful not to sob loudly and frighten Mica.

"Did Sean say something dumb that made you sad?" Leslie's fists clenched. "If he did, I'll punch him in the throat for you."

Ava laughed, the sound catching on a sob. "No. He's been perfect. It's me."

"Hold that thought." Leslie jumped up to grab a couple of mugs and filled them with the fragrant brew. She set them down on the table and took her seat again. "Now, elaborate, dear. I can't read your mind. It was you? How so? Did he take advantage of you? Make you mad? Hurt your feelings?"

Ava stared at Leslie for a long moment, searching for the words that would describe just what she was feeling. Tears welled up in her eyes and trickled down her cheeks. "I don't know. All I know is I have to break it off with him."

"Why?" Leslie asked. "I thought you two were getting along so well. And he's so good with Mica. Why would you want to break things off?"

"It's not what we both said we wanted. I can't put Mica in a situation where she could potentially be miserable. And we both said we weren't in it for the long haul. The problem is, the more I'm with him, the more I want to be with him. I have to break it off now, before someone gets hurt."

Leslie smiled gently. "Is that someone you, Ava?" She laid her hand over Ava's. "Are you afraid of being hurt? That you might be falling in love and he'll leave?"

"No." Ava shook her head vehemently.

Leslie's eyebrow cocked. The woman saw right through her.

Ava nodded. "Yes. I can't see him again. It's not fair to Mica, and it'll only be harder the longer this drags on. I already feel awful about it."

"Oh, sweetie, you're falling in love."

"No, that's impossible," Ava frowned. "I've only

met the man. We've only been together two nights. People don't fall in love that fast. It takes years."

"Like it did for you and Michael?" Leslie asked, her tone quiet.

"Yes. We knew each other for years before we knew we were in love and wanted to marry."

"Have you never heard of love at first sight?" Leslie asked.

Ava grimaced. "Surely, you don't believe in it. That's purely lust. Once the lust wears off, what do you have? Nothing. And he'll have no reason to stay."

"Have you ever thought that maybe you're feeling the way you are because you and Sean are perfect for each other? BODS matched you for a reason. I didn't do anything to influence the system. It was all about what you and Sean entered in your preferences."

Ava pressed her hands to her cheeks. "He doesn't want a lasting relationship. I don't want Mica to get too attached. It will break her heart when he leaves."

"What if he doesn't leave?"

"I can't take that chance."

"But what if he doesn't?"

"Then he'll come to regret that he's stuck in a relationship he never wanted, and he could take it out on Mica. I can't risk that. I've lived through that kind of hell. I won't put Mica through it."

Leslie leaned forward, a frown pressing her eyebrows together. "Sean isn't your stepfather, Ava."

"My mother and stepfather had to have loved

each other when they first met. The problem was he could never accept a child that wasn't his blood. It's hard for any man."

"I repeat, Sean is not like your stepfather." Leslie drew in a deep breath. "Do yourself a favor and don't make any rash decisions. We're supposed to go out tonight with the gang."

"I can't go," Ava said, shaking her head.

"You need to go and talk things over with Sean. See if he's had a change of heart about the whole 'no relationship' thing."

Ava shook her head. "I can't. He was just as adamant about it as I was. Even if he has changed his mind, that doesn't mean he wants a relationship involving a woman with a small child."

"I don't know, he was really good with Mica at the fair last night. And she's taken a shine to him."

Ava flung her hands in the air. "Exactly. This will only hurt Mica. I have to break it off with Sean before things get worse."

A sound in the hallway outside the kitchen made Ava freeze. She rose from her chair and hurried to see if Mica was eavesdropping on their quiet conversation.

The hallway was empty.

Leslie came to stand beside Ava, a worried frown denting her brow. "Do you think she heard us talking?"

Ava shook her head. "I hope not. I don't think

she'd understand all of it, even if she did." She walked down the hallway to Mica's room. The door was closed.

She opened it and looked inside.

Mica sat on her little bed, hugging her stuffed bunny.

"Are you okay, Mica?" Ava asked.

Mica nodded and hugged her bunny tighter. "I missed my bunny."

Ava smiled. "I missed my Mica." She crossed to her daughter, bent and gave her a big hug. "I love you, sweetie."

Mica flung her arms around Ava's neck and squeezed hard. "I love you too, Mama."

"I'll be in the kitchen if you get hungry," Ava said and left the door to Mica's room open as she left and returned to the kitchen.

"Is she okay?" Leslie asked.

"She's fine," Ava said.

"I need to go. But I want you to think about it before you do anything." Leslie hugged Ava. "Whatever happens, I only want to see you and Mica happy. And if you want to break it off, do it tonight when we're all out at the Ugly Stick. I can take you home afterward."

Ava hugged her friend. "Thanks. You're a good friend."

"I love you like a sister." Leslie hugged her again and left the house.

Ava could have spent the day doing laundry and cleaning house, but she didn't want to sit around and think anymore. Every time she did, she thought about what she needed to do and started crying.

She'd read online that Austin was having a parade for veterans in the downtown area. Supporting the troops was a much better use of her time than moping around the house in anticipation of breaking it off with a man she could so very easily fall in love with.

"Mica, put on your shoes," she called out. "We're going to a parade."

SEAN WOKE that morning and rolled over to love on the woman who'd rocked his world the night before.

The pillow beside him was cold and empty.

He sat up and listened for sounds of Ava moving about his massive penthouse.

Silence reigned.

Throwing back the comforter, he leaped out of bed and made a quick pass through the apartment, knowing it was in vain. Her clothes and shoes were nowhere to be found.

Ava had left sometime in the early hours of the morning.

He worried that a lone woman in the dark wasn't safe in the downtown area. With a glance at the clock on the microwave, he whistled. Ten-thirty? Hell, she could have left during the daylight for all he knew. How had he actually slept for so long? He never stayed in bed past six in the morning.

Sean headed for the shower, making a detour through the living room to snag his cellphone. He dialed Leslie's number. She was supposed to drop off Mica at ten and would have seen Ava in the process.

Leslie answered on the first ring. "What did you do to Ava to make her cry?" she asked without preamble.

His heart skipped several beats. "Ava was crying? Why?"

"She's convinced she needs to break it off with you. I just spent the last thirty minutes mopping up her tears. I repeat, what did you do to make her cry?"

"I have no idea." Sean dropped onto the sofa, his gut knotting at the thought of Ava in tears. "What did she say?"

"That you two were only supposed to be dating, and she couldn't risk hurting Mica when you guys split up. Did you tell her that you were going to break it off with her soon?"

"No. In fact, we have a date tonight," Sean said. "I thought the evening went really well. I don't know what changed from the time she went to sleep to the time I woke up."

"Oh, Lord. You did it, didn't you?"

His cheeks heated. "I don't know what you're talking about."

"You made love to her, didn't you?"

"I don't know what business it is of yours what Ava and I did last night."

"Don't you see?"

He flung his free hand in the air. "What are you talking about? I don't see anything."

"You made love. Holy hell, you made love too soon. Now she thinks she has to break it off because she's afraid of falling in love with you. You didn't give her enough time."

"Time for what?"

"She married her best friend from grade school. They knew each other for years before they dated and married after high school. That's why she thinks falling in love is a long process."

"Who's falling in love?" Sean's heart beat faster at the thought. Falling in love? Was Ava falling in love with him?

Hell, was he falling in love with Ava? Was that why she was constantly in his thoughts? Everywhere he looked, he saw her in something. The sky was the color of her eyes. Every blonde he passed made him look twice in hopes it was her.

"Sean? Are you still there?"

"Yeah." He shook his head to clear it of all the images he'd stored in his memory of Ava at the steak restaurant, Ava and Mica on the Ferris wheel—Ava in his bed, her hair splayed out across the pillow. "I'm here," he murmured.

"Oh, boy. You two are a case. You're falling in love and fighting it all the way," Leslie said. "BODS put you two together for a reason. You're a perfect match. Why are you making it difficult on yourselves?"

"I'm not falling in love," Sean said, though his tone wasn't all that convincing.

"Whatever," Leslie said, dismissively. "What are you going to do to keep her?" She paused. "You want to keep her in your life, don't you?"

"Yes," he answered before he could think too hard. "Yes," he repeated, knowing it was what he wanted. "But am I the right guy for her? She's special, and Mica is a terrific kid. I don't want to screw her up with my crappy track record."

"What track record?" Leslie demanded.

"My childhood wasn't perfect. My father was a bad example of what a dad should be. I don't have the skills to be a good father."

"You were wonderful with Mica at the fair. Why do you think you're not daddy material? You are not your father. You learned what a bad father is, and you'll never let a child suffer like you did."

"Mica deserves a good man."

"Sean, you're a good man. You need to cut yourself some slack. You'll make a great father."

"You're assuming Ava and Mica want a man in their lives. And you're assuming I'm falling in love with them." He shook his head, though Leslie couldn't see him do it. "We've only been out twice."

"And you hit it off immediately. You're made for each other. You just have to get Ava to give you guys time to make her feel comfortable that you're not going to bug out of their lives."

"But what if she doesn't want me in her and Mica's lives? I can't stalk her. She'll get a restraining order."

"I don't know what to tell you. Whatever you do, you need to get her to go out with you again. And again, until she learns that you're in it for the long haul."

"How do I do that? What if she calls to say she's not going to go out with me tonight?"

"Don't answer the phone," Leslie said.

"What?"

"If you don't answer the phone, she can't cancel on you."

"She could leave a message or text."

"Show up at her door at the agreed-on time like you never got a message." Leslie sighed. "Just get her to go out with you again. You can't let this end. She's in love with you. I just know it."

"How do you know it?"

"A woman doesn't cry that many tears over a man she doesn't love," Leslie said. "You have to convince her that everything will be okay. I have to go. You're a smart man. You wouldn't be a billionaire if you weren't. Figure it out." Leslie ended the call, leaving Sean with a knot the size of Texas in his gut.

Ava wanted to break it off with him.

No way. No freakin' way.

His cellphone rang. Thinking it might be Leslie again, he had his thumb hovering over the receiver button and almost pressed it when he saw the caller ID.

Ava.

Every instinct inside him urged him to take the call. Leslie's words echoed in his mind. He ignored the call and ducked into the shower. He had an engagement to make that day that had been planned for quite some time, or he would have skipped it and run over to Ava's house.

It was a good thing he had that engagement. He couldn't go to Ava's house until it was time for their date. She had promised to cook dinner for him.

Surely, she'd go ahead with their plans if she couldn't talk with him long enough to cancel the date.

Either way, he was showing up at her house at six-thirty that evening. Whether she let him through the door or not was completely up in the air.

All he knew was that he had to try. Deep in his heart he knew that Ava was worth the effort. Ava and Mica. The two had found a way into his heart, filling a void he'd never known he had. He'd be damned if he'd let them slip away.

CHAPTER 9

AVA AND MICA arrived thirty minutes early to the street where the parade would take place to get good spots to view the procession.

She'd purchased a small American flag for each of them to wave as the veterans passed by.

A motorcycle gang, wearing black leather jackets and red, white and blue do-rags, fell in beside her and Mica.

At first, Ava was apprehensive, until one of the bikers smiled and handed Mica a stuffed bear with a black leather vest like the one he wore.

Mica thanked him and grinned up at her mother. "Look what the nice man gave me."

Ava thanked him. The gang was a good reminder to her not to judge people based on what they wore. They were there to support the veterans, just like her and Mica.

The parade began with an Army color guard, carrying the American and Texas flags. They stopped in front of the viewing stand and waited for the University of Texas marching band to fall in behind them. Once they came to a stop, they all faced the stands to play the Star-Spangled Banner while the Texas flag was lowered, and the American flag waved in the breeze.

Ava stood proud and sang the national anthem with the crowd of onlookers.

After the final note played, the marching band led the procession down the street to a medley of songs representing the different branches of service.

A group of veterans on motorcycles rolled slowly by with flags flying from the backs of their bikes. They were followed by a troop of veterans on horseback, each sporting an American flag on a pole.

An Air Force Unit marched by in their blue uniforms, all in step, all facing forward as they marched to the beat of the man calling cadence.

A group of men in camouflage uniforms walked by, pushing the wheelchairs of aged and disabled veterans. Many of those disabled veterans wore the purple hearts they'd been awarded for their injuries sustained in combat.

One of the men walked close to where Ava and Mica were standing, pushing a wheelchair.

Before Ava could react, Mica shouted, "Mr.

Decker. It's Mr. Decker." She ran into the street and hurled herself at the man in the military uniform.

Sean let go of the wheelchair with one hand and caught Mica.

"Mica!" Ava ran after her daughter, only to discover the man who'd occupied all of her thoughts for the past week held Mica in one arm, while he continued to push the wheelchair of the elderly disabled veteran.

"Hey," he said. "If I'd known you wanted to help, I would have invited you to come along."

"Can I? Can I help push?" Mica clapped her hands.

"I don't see why not." He looked across at Ava. "As long as your mother is okay with it."

"Mama? May I?" Mica pressed her hands together as if in prayer. "Please."

Ava frowned. "Are you sure it's all right? It looks like only military personnel are doing the job."

"I'm sure Sergeant Stanley would much rather have two pretty girls push his chair than me." Sean leaned over the man in the chair. "Am I right, Sergeant Stanley?" he asked, practically yelling at the man so that he could hear.

"Oh, yes. Yes. Pretty girls." He winked at Ava and Mica. "Much better."

Sean set Mica on her feet.

Ava's daughter handed the little flag she'd been

holding to the old man in the chair, making him smile.

She moved to the back of the chair and reached up to the handles.

With Sean's help, she pushed the chair down the street, keeping pace with the parade for the first few blocks. When she grew tired, Sergeant Stanley offered to let her ride with him, which delighted Mica.

Ava marched alongside Sean, conflicted once again by her desire to keep distance between Mica and Sean and her desire to see more of the man. If she was the only one with anything to risk, she might take her chances and ride the wave to the end. But her decisions impacted her daughter. She couldn't let her selfish desires break Mica's heart.

Sean had stated up front that he wasn't into long relationships. And nowhere in the list of preferences had he said he wanted to play father to his date's child. If he did decide to take on both of them, how soon would it be before he began to resent his ready-made family?

Ava's stepfather hadn't always been mean. The anger and resentment seemed to have built over the years, until all he ever did was find fault with her and yell whenever she came into the room.

When the parade came to an end, Ava thanked the disabled veterans for their service and sacrifice. Then she turned to Sean with every intention of calling off their night of dinner and dancing.

"Sean, I—"

Sean held up a finger. "Sorry. I hate to cut you off, but I need to get Sergeant Stanley to the van taking the veterans back to the home." He picked up Mica and hugged her close. "Keep an eye on your mother. Hold her hand so that she doesn't get lost in the crowd."

Mica nodded, her face serious. "I will." She wrapped her arms around his neck and hugged him tight. "Thank you for your service," she said, mimicking what others had said all along the way. "I love you, Mr. Decker."

Ava's heart squeezed hard in her chest. She had to end their connection. Mica was entirely too attached to the man already.

"Sean, we really need to talk," Ava said.

He'd turned Mr. Stanley around and started for the exit. "I'll see you at six-thirty, tonight," he called out over his shoulder. "I'm bringing the wine."

"About that, Mr. Decker," Ava called out, "I don't think it's a good—"

Sean was halfway to the parking lot. He glanced over his shoulder. "Did you say something?" he shouted over the noise of the crowd dispersing.

"I'm not sure it's a good idea—"

He cupped a hand to his ear. "Can't hear you. I'm

riding back to the care center. I'll see you for dinner at six-thirty."

Then he was gone.

Ava's intention to call off that evening's dinner and dancing had been as effective as spitting in the wind. She still had a date, and her date was expecting a home-cooked meal.

Not that she minded cooking, but it meant spending more time with the man she was having difficulty letting go. And she wasn't sure she had a babysitter for the evening. She didn't want Mica to get too used to having Sean around. She already had it in her head that he was going to be her new daddy.

Mica took her hand and stared up at her with rounded eyes. "Daddy—Mr. Decker's coming for dinner?" A smile wreathed her face. She let go of Ava's hand and clapped hers together, hopping up and down. "Yay! Can we make cupcakes for dessert?"

So much for getting a babysitter for dinner. If she told Mica she couldn't stay for dinner, the child would be heartbroken.

With a sigh, Ava nodded. "We can make cupcakes. But don't get used to having Mr. Decker around. He's a busy man."

"I know," Mica said, slipping her hand back in Ava's. "But he's having dinner with us tonight. And we're making cupcakes for dessert."

Ava and Mica walked back to where she'd parked her car, got in and went to the grocery store for the ingredients for lasagna and cupcakes. She picked up a loaf of French bread and salad ingredients. If she was going to make dinner for her last date, she'd do it right. Afterward, she'd break it to Sean that they couldn't see each other again.

With a head of iceberg lettuce in her hand, she froze, her heart constricting. She tossed the lettuce into the cart, added leaf spinach, tomatoes and green onions, fighting back tears.

"What's wrong, Mama?" Mica asked.

"Nothing, sweetie," she said, her voice catching on a sob. She swallowed hard to hold it back.

Mica reached for her hand. "Why are you crying?"

Ava pasted a smile on her face and pointed to the green onions. "Onions always make me cry."

"Then why do you get them?"

"I don't know," Ava said. "What kind of cake mix do we want for our cupcakes?" she asked, deflecting Mica's attention from her to dessert.

"Chocolate with strawberry frosting and sprinkles." Mica skipped ahead to the baked goods aisles and selected the mix, frosting and colorful candy sprinkles. With the dessert ingredients in the cart, they headed for check out and home.

Ava and Mica spent the afternoon cooking, decorating cupcakes and dancing in the kitchen to eighties music. By six-thirty, they had two dozen cupcakes, beautifully decorated, a lasagna, fresh out of the oven and smelling divine, and garlic French bread toasting under the broiler.

Ava had chosen a denim skirt, a plaid blouse knotted at the waist and cowboy boots to wear. She'd pulled her long blond hair up into a messy bun, letting loose tendrils fall down around her ears.

She figured, even if she was going to break up the man, she might as well look good while she did it. Looking your best helped build confidence, right? A lump lodged in her throat. She'd miss seeing him and the anticipation of being together.

Mica had chosen her best pink dress and white patent leather shoes. Ava had French-braided her hair and added a fat pink bow to match her dress.

She hated that her daughter would be sad when Sean didn't return for more dinners at their little house. Mica and Ava would miss him. But Sean would move on. He was a wealthy man. He would have no trouble finding a willing woman to fill the gap.

Ava's fingernails dug into her palms. But would that woman know what a find she had in Sean? And by find, it wouldn't have anything to do with the amount of money he had in his bank account or the number of houses or penthouses he owned.

Sean was rich with good friends, a warm heart and a love for his fellow military veterans. He volunteered with the disabled. Hell, he rescued kittens from highways. Yes, she'd seen the news report of the backed-up traffic and the image of a man holding a small kitten in the middle of a busy highway.

Sean was also kind to fatherless children. Well, he was kind to Mica, anyway. The man hadn't had to read a book to her the first time they'd met or escort her through the country fair, winning prizes and holding her hand on the Ferris wheel.

He'd make a good dad, despite his concern that he hadn't been raised that way. Sean had learned from his old man's mistakes. He wouldn't repeat them.

Then why was she in such a hurry to ditch him?

Ava retrieved the garlic bread from the oven before she burned it and set it on the counter.

"He's here! He's here!" Mica came running into the kitchen, her eyes alight with excitement.

Ava turned off the oven, took Mica's hand and let her lead her to the front door.

Her love for Mica was the reason she had to break it off with Sean. He'd leave soon enough, when he'd had enough of dating a woman with a small child.

Sean had been clear that he didn't want to marry. The sooner they stopped seeing each other, the sooner Ava and Mica could start mending their broken hearts.

The doorbell rang as Ava admitted to herself that she would have to work on her own broken heart. For she'd done the worst thing imaginable. She'd fallen in love with a man who wasn't available.

Mica pulled open the door and flung herself at Sean. "You came!"

He laughed and picked her up in one arm, while holding a bouquet of roses in his other hand. "Of course, I came." He gave her a loud kiss on her cheek and handed the flowers to Ava. "These are for you."

Ava took the flowers automatically, still in shock from her internal revelation.

Sean reached into his pocket and pulled out a tiny stuffed purple unicorn. "And this is for you. I figured Reggie would be lonely and in need of a friend."

Mica took the little unicorn. "Thank you," she said and hugged Sean so tightly around the neck, Ava worried the man couldn't breathe.

Sean grinned and inhaled deeply. "Something smells really good."

"Cupcakes!" Mica said. She wiggled in Sean's arms until he set her on her feet. Grabbing his hand, she dragged him through the house and into the tiny kitchen. "We made chocolate cupcakes with strawberry frosting and sprinkles just for you."

"My favorite," Sean said. "I love sprinkles."

"I told you he would," Mica called out to her mother.

Ava buried her face in the roses and breathed in the fragrance, letting it calm her storm of her emotions.

She followed the sound of her daughter talking nonstop to Sean as she showed him the cupcakes, the lasagna, the French bread and the table set neatly with flatware and napkins.

Mica said, "I helped set the table and folded the napkins."

"You did a wonderful job," Sean said. He stepped around Mica and took the bouquet of flowers from Ava. "Do you have a vase?"

Ava nodded, suddenly shy with the man she'd made passionate love to the night before. He'd seen her naked, and he acted as if it was as natural as breathing to see her fully clothed again.

Her head spinning with a wild array of thoughts and images of a naked Sean, lying in bed, Ava opened one cabinet door after the other looking for… What was it she was looking for?

Oh, yes. A vase.

Finally, she came across a vase she'd saved from when Leslie and Emma had sent her flowers for her birthday. She filled it halfway full of water and set it on the counter.

Sean joined her in front of the vase and helped her settle the stems in the water, one at a time.

Several times, their hands touched, sending sparks of electricity shooting through her arm into her chest and down to heat her core.

When the last rose was placed in the vase, Ava didn't trust herself to carry it to the table.

"Let me," Sean said, his voice a low rumble in her

ear, the way it had been the night before when he'd been kissing the side of her neck.

A shiver of awareness rippled across her skin. Ava quickly stepped away from Sean. She had to keep her distance, or she'd fall under his spell and forget what she had to do at the end of the meal.

Sean carried the flowers to the table and set them at one end, leaving the center for the food.

He returned to the stove to carry the lasagna to the table. Ava brought the salad, and Mica carried the basket of garlic bread.

When everything was on the table, Sean frowned. "I forgot one thing. I'll be right back."

He left the kitchen, giving Ava a chance to breathe for a moment.

Mica sniffed the roses. "When a daddy gives a mommy roses, it means he loves her." She glanced up at Ava and smiled.

Ava's heart contracted. If only Mica's statement were true.

Sean reappeared a moment later, carrying what appeared to be a wine bottle. "I thought we could celebrate with a little bubbly."

Mica clapped her hands. "I like bubbles."

"None for you, miss," Ava said.

"Mica can have some. It's sparkling grape juice. Nonalcoholic. I didn't want to leave her out of the fun." He peeled the foil off the top of the cork and popped it open.

Mica squealed and giggled.

"Do you have wine or champagne glasses?" he asked.

Ava shook her head. "No," she said. "We keep it pretty simple around here. "What you see is our best." And up against what he had in his penthouse, it was a poor comparison. Ava straightened her shoulders. But it was hers and she was making it on her own, with a child.

"These glasses are perfect," he said and poured sparkling liquid into the glasses. When he was done, he held Mica's chair for her and spread her napkin on her lap. Then he held Ava's.

She took her seat, a flutter of nerves shooting out from where his knuckles brushed her back.

Sean made certain Mica was served first with a square of lasagna, some salad and a piece of the bread before he passed the items to Ava.

She helped herself to the food, wondering how she'd ever swallow any of it. Her throat was so tight, she could barely breathe.

"Would you mind if I said a blessing?" Sean asked.

Ava shook her head. "Please."

"Let's hold hands," he said.

Sean took Mica's hand and gathered Ava's in the other.

Her heart beat so fast, she was sure he could feel her pulse in her fingers.

"Lord, please keep our military personnel safe and

bring them home unharmed," he started. "Help the hungry find the food they need, protect the children and guide us in making the decisions that will lead us to happiness."

Sean's hand tightened on hers as he made that final statement.

Ava opened her eyes enough to look at the way his fingers curled around hers. Was any of his message directed toward her?

"Bless the food we are about to eat and the people who prepared it. Thank you for all our blessings. Amen."

Mica and Ava murmured another amen.

Sean held onto her hand a moment longer, before releasing it. "Thank you for sharing your dinner with me," he said. "I can't think of two people I'd rather have dinner with more." He winked at Mica and turned a gentle smile toward Ava. "I mean that."

Mica leaned toward her mother with her hand cupping her mouth. "See? I was right."

Sean looked from Mica to Ava and back. "Right about what?"

Ava frowned at Mica.

"Roses mean—"

"That's enough, Mica. Eat your salad before you eat anything else," Ava said, her voice a little harsher than she'd intended.

"Roses mean what?" Sean asked.

"Nothing," Ava said. "Would you like a piece of garlic bread?"

The time was quickly getting near for her to tell Sean they couldn't see each other again.

Ava couldn't swallow past the lump in her throat. This dating thing had turned out to be a lot harder than she'd anticipated.

She wished she'd never signed onto the BODS system.

As she stared across the table at Sean, she shook her head. If she hadn't, she wouldn't have met Sean, and she wouldn't have known she could fall in love again.

CHAPTER 10

SEAN ACCEPTED the garlic toast and ate the lasagna, smiled and chatted with Mica. All the while, he could sense the tension in the air between himself and Ava.

She didn't touch her food, and she jumped every time he touched her.

Had he ruined everything by making love to her too soon as Leslie had mentioned?

The night had been incredible…to him. Had it not been as good for Ava? Was she having major regrets?

All Sean knew was that he had to get her past this bump in their dating road. He wanted to see her again. And again. Hell, he wanted her in his life.

His gaze went to little Mica who had tucked her napkin into the collar of her dress to keep from getting marinara sauce on her good clothes.

She was a precious little girl. Any man would be proud to have her as a daughter.

Sean loved that she was happy to see him and that she'd hugged him around the neck so tightly he couldn't breathe. He could imagine coming home to her every day.

Yeah, she wouldn't always be so happy to see him, and teenage years would be difficult, but she'd grow into a beautiful young woman like her mother and be a friend, if he played his cards right and loved her as if she were his own. He'd never be mean to a child. He'd seen the damage it had done to him and his brother.

He'd thought they'd worked past it until his brother returned from multiple deployments, got out of the military and returned to the only place he'd known as home. Sean had still been deployed when Patrick had returned, or he might have seen what was happening with his brother.

He might have saved him from the self-loathing spiral he'd fallen into.

By the time Sean got back Stateside, Patrick was deep into drugs. He'd never made the transition back to civilian life. How could he? The only civilian life he'd known was with an abusive father.

Sean had tried to get Patrick the help he'd needed, but his brother had refused. He hadn't thought he had a problem and had resented Sean's interference.

Within a week of his return, Sean received a phone call from his father stating Patrick had committed suicide. The old man hadn't expressed any words of sorrow or regret. Just bald facts. Then, he'd abruptly ended the call.

Sean had attended Patrick's funeral. His father had not. The call had been the last time he'd heard from his father, and he'd made no attempt to contact him, ever again.

"Do you want a cupcake now?" Mica asked, pulling him out of memories and back to the table with the two young ladies Sean was finding harder and harder to resist.

"I'd love one," he said. When he started to get up, Mica touched his arm.

"I'll get them," she said.

She skipped across the kitchen and took her time to select the best of cupcakes.

Ava leaned forward. "We need to talk."

Sean forced a smile. "Can we wait until after the cupcakes?"

Mica returned, carrying two. She had icing on her fingers as she handed one to her mother and one to Sean. "I gave you the one with the most sprinkles," she said with a smile, then turned and ran back to get a cupcake for herself.

Sean made a big show of admiring the cupcake. "This is the most beautiful cupcake I've ever seen. Did you put the sprinkles on it?"

Mica nodded and licked the icing off hers, getting a smudge of the pink frosting on her nose. "Me and Mama made them."

"I believe you're as sweet as this cupcake," he said and wiped the frosting off with his napkin. Then he bit into the sweet and moaned. "Mmm. It tastes as good as it looks."

"Mama says if you cook with love, it will always taste good," Mica bit into her cupcake.

Sean raised his eyebrows and shot a glance at Ava. "Is that so?"

She shrugged. "My mother used to tell me that. I guess it's habit."

Sean turned back to Mica. "I believe there's a whole lot of love in this cupcake, because it's delicious."

Mica giggled and ate another bite of her cupcake.

When Sean had finished his dessert, he helped carry their plates to the sink, making note of the fact Ava didn't have a dishwasher. "I'll wash, you dry?" he offered.

"We can leave them in the sink. I'll wash them later," she said.

"I insist. I can't leave you with all these dishes when you did all the cooking." Sean filled the sink with soapy water and did something he hadn't done since he'd been a kid. He washed dishes by hand.

Ava sighed, took up a dish towel and dried, putting the plates and cutlery away as she did.

When the kitchen had been set to rights, Ava bent to Mica. "Why don't you go play in your room for a little while. Mr. Decker and I need a little adult time."

Mica frowned. "But I want to stay and visit with Mr. Decker."

Ava didn't argue. She raised her brow and crossed her arms over her chest.

Mica must have known that look, because her shoulders slumped, and she turned toward the door. She was halfway through the door when she spun and glared at her mother. "Don't say anything to make him go away."

Ava blinked, her arms dropping to her sides. "Mica."

"Promise," Mica said, tears filling her eyes. "Please."

Sean wanted to take Mica in his arms and hug the tears away and reassure her that he wasn't going anywhere. But he couldn't. Ava held all the cards in this situation. If he didn't get her approval, he was out.

Ava went to her daughter and pulled her into her arms for a quick hug. "Oh, baby, we'll talk in a few minutes. Right now, I need to see Mr. Decker alone."

"Promise," she whispered.

Ava didn't. "We'll talk in a minute."

Mica stepped out her mother's arms and went to Sean.

He knelt to wrap his arms around her. "Hey, sweetie."

"Don't go away," she whispered in his ear. "I love you."

Sean hugged her and whispered back in her ear. "I love you, too." Louder, he said, "You need to do as your mother said, Mica."

He wanted to be a part of the little girl's life. He wanted to be a part of her mother's life. They had quickly shown him what he'd been missing, and he didn't want to let go.

"It'll be all right," he said, hoping he was correct.

Mica stepped back, her lip trembling. "No, it won't." And she ran down the hall to her room, slamming the door behind her.

"That didn't go over well," Ava muttered. "Look, we might as well get down to the nitty gritty." She drew in a deep breath.

"Before you say anything, would you answer something for me?"

She frowned. "Okay."

"About last night...did I do anything to make you mad, hurt your feelings, or make you hate me?" He took her hands in his. "Because, from my point of view, it was the best night of my life. I'd hate to think you didn't feel the same." He brought her fingers to his lips and kissed the tips.

For a moment, he thought Ava was going to cry; her brow puckered, and her eyes filled. "No. You didn't. It was the most incredibly perfect night for me."

At her words, relief washed over Sean. As long as he hadn't done anything to ruin his chances with her, he could figure out whatever it was that was bothering her.

He hoped.

Ava stared down at where he held her hands. "From the beginning, we agreed that we didn't want a long-term relationship."

Sean stiffened. In the beginning, that was exactly what he'd wanted. But he'd since changed his mind. He'd met and fallen in love with Ava and Mica. There was no going back on that.

Ava pulled her hands free and turned away. "I never meant for you to meet Mica," she said quietly. "We were supposed to date and be done. No commitment. No demands." Her voice grew shaky.

His gut knotted. She was pulling away from him. Like Leslie had said, she was about to cut him loose. He couldn't let that happen.

Sean closed the distance between them and laid his hands on her shoulders. "What if we changed our minds?"

She leaned her back against his chest and was silent for a long moment. Then she said, "We can't go back on our agreement. Mica is my world. I couldn't live with myself if she was hurt because of my selfishness."

"Why would dating me be selfish? I would gladly bring Mica along." He massaged her shoulders, wanting to kiss her and make her see how much he cared. "She's an awesome kid."

Ava's chest expanded on a deep breath. Then she pushed away from him and spun to face him. "That's just it. I don't want *any* man near my daughter. It isn't fair giving her unrealistic expectations. She wants a daddy. And just in the few times she's been with you, she's set her heart on you." She waved her hand. "So, we can't see each other anymore. We're done. You can't come back here. It's too confusing for Mica." The tears slipped from her eyes and trailed down her cheeks. "It's too confusing for me," she murmured.

Her tears tore at Sean's heart. He reached out and took her into his arms.

She tried to resist but soon gave up and wrapped her arms around his waist. Ava buried her face in his shirt and sobbed.

He let her cry, smoothing her hair back from her face. "Shh, sweetheart, it's going to be all right."

"No, it's not," she said. "Mica's going to get hurt when you leave. It might as well be sooner than later. You have to go." She straightened and pressed her hands against his chest. "Now."

"Is that what you really want?" he asked. He touched a finger to her chin and lifted it, forcing her to face him. "Is that what you want?"

"For Mica, yes," she whispered.

He leaned down and brushed his lips across hers. "What about for you?"

The tears flooded her cheeks. "What I want doesn't matter," she said, her voice choking on a sob.

"You're wrong, Ava. What you want matters to me." He kissed her again. "I'll go if you don't want me. If you want me, all you have to do is say so."

She looked up into his face through her tear-soaked blue eyes and bit down on her trembling lip.

He nodded and stepped back, letting his arms fall to his sides. "Before I leave, you need to know this."

Sean stood straight, his shoulders back, his fists clenched, all in an attempt to hold himself together. "I wouldn't be here now, if I didn't care about you. I wouldn't have come to dinner with you and Mica, if I didn't care about Mica."

He laughed, the sound hollow with his fear of losing her and the little girl who'd won his heart. "I was the last person in the world who believed in love at first sight and happily-ever-afters. But you and Mica have shown me what I've been missing all of my damned life." He stepped up to her and gripped her arms hard. "Do you want to know what that is?"

She dragged in a deep breath and nodded.

"You showed me what love could be. That's right. I said the word *love*. Because that's what this is. And Mica showed me I wasn't my father, and that I had something to give to a child…" He touched his fist to his chest. "My heart."

He let go of her arm. "If you're set on booting me out of your life and Mica's life, I'll go. But you know where I live. When you realize it wasn't me who left, you know where to find me. I don't want to leave. I want to stay and be a permanent part of your lives."

He waited for her to say something. When she didn't, he spun on a booted heel and left the kitchen, left the house and climbed into his truck, his heart shattering into a million pieces.

How could it be? He hadn't known her that long.

But it was long enough. His heart knew her... knew the truth. He loved Ava and Mica.

Yet, Ava had made it clear. She didn't want him in her life. Mica or no Mica. Their short affair hadn't meant as much to her as it had to him. The sooner he accepted that, the better off he would be.

AVA STOOD as if rooted to the floor, her entire world crumbling around her. She'd just sent Sean away when, in her heart, it was the last thing she'd wanted to do. In the few short days she'd known him, she'd fallen head over heels in love with the man.

How could that be? No one fell in love that fast.

Or did they, and she was the exception? Her love for Michael had been a slow build from friend to lover to husband. She'd thought that was the only way to fall in love.

Ava pressed her hands to her damp cheeks, every instinct in her mind and body urging her to go after Sean.

He said he wanted to be part of her life. And

he'd included Mica. He understood they were a package deal. He was a good man who saved kittens and volunteered with veterans. Why would he lie to her?

The truth hit her square in the gut.

"He wouldn't lie," she said out loud. "He wouldn't."

She took one step, then another, her feet carrying her of their own accord out of the kitchen and across the living room. Then she was running out the front door.

Sean had backed out of the driveway and was pulling away.

"Sean!" she yelled and ran after the truck as he drove away.

He didn't stop until he reached the stop sign on the corner. By then, he was too far ahead for Ava to catch up to him.

She leaned against the neighbor's mailbox, sobbing, her eyes too filled with tears to see anything.

The rumble of a vehicle's engine sounded near her.

Ava didn't move. She didn't care if someone ran over her at that moment. She'd just made the biggest mistake of her life by sending away the man she loved.

Hands gripped her arms and turned her.

Ava batted at the hands. "I'll move. You don't have to manhandle me. It's just a stupid mailbox."

"Ava," a voice said through her sobs. "Sweetheart."

She glanced up at the man holding her and cried ever harder. "You left."

"You told me to go," he said, kissing the tip of her damp nose. "I didn't want to."

"I don't want you to go. I was wrong. I do believe in love at first sight. I love you, Sean Decker." Ava wrapped her arms around his neck and pulled him down to kiss her.

It took her a moment to realize Sean had stiffened.

"Uh, sweetheart," he said and pushed her to arm's length. "You need to know something else."

She frowned, a bad feeling eating away at her happiness. "What?"

His lips twisted into a grimace. "I haven't been completely truthful with you."

She stepped back, afraid. So afraid he would say he didn't really love her or Mica. Or that he was already married. "What is it? You can tell me."

"My name isn't Sean Decker."

Her brow dipped lower. "You're not Sean Decker?" She shook her head. "Then who are you?"

"My real name is Sean, and my call name in the Navy was Decker. But my last name is O'Leary. I'm Sean O'Leary." He waited for her response.

She shrugged. "So? I get it that you didn't want to use your real name in the BODS system. As long as you still love me and Mica, and that you're not married to two other women, I'm okay with that. You're still the same man."

He laughed and pulled her into his arms. "You really don't know who Sean O'Leary is?"

She leaned up on her toes and kissed his lips. "Yes, I do. You're an amazing man who has the good sense to love me and my daughter. Speaking of which, we need to get back to the house. Mica wasn't too happy with the way I left things."

Sean took Ava's hand and led her back to the little cottage Ava called home. "I can't believe you don't know who Sean O'Leary is."

She looked up at him, her eyes narrowing. "Should I? You're not wanted or anything, are you?" She shook her head. "No. Leslie's clients are vetted and go through a background check before she lets them into her system." She canted her head to one side. "What should I know that I obviously don't?"

He laughed. "Just that I love you. And I love Mica." They hurried up the steps and in through the open door. "I can't believe you came running after my truck."

She snorted. "I can't believe you left."

"You told me to." He grinned. "Truth is…I was going to drive around the block and come back to talk sense into you."

"Thankfully, I came to the right conclusion on my own." She stopped him in front of Mica's room and kissed him again.

"I could get used to kissing you," she said.

"Good, because I plan on doing it a lot." He pulled her close and deepened the kiss, until her toes curled, and she forgot she needed to breathe.

When his mouth left hers, he leaned his forehead against hers. "Is it too early to talk about marriage?"

She laughed. "We can't get married soon enough, in my books. At least then, you won't be able to leave us."

Sean frowned and stood back a step. "I want you to know, I take marriage very seriously."

She looked up into his grave eyes and knew the truth.

"I'm in it for the long haul. Once I commit, I'll do everything in my power to make it work."

She smiled. "Are you asking me to commit?"

He nodded. "I am."

"I will," she said. "And you? Are you ready to commit?"

"I am, and I will."

Her cheeks heated and her heart fluttered. "Should we kiss on it?"

"Absolutely." Once again, he kissed her until she was breathless.

When they broke apart, she brushed the hair out of her face and drew air into her lungs. "Should we tell Mica?"

"I'd love to."

"She'll be thrilled to be getting the daddy of her

choice." Ava reached for the door handle, twisted it and flung it open. "Mica, I have good news—"

Her words fell on an empty room.

A breeze fluttered the light pink curtains at the open window.

Mica was gone.

CHAPTER 11

Sean ran out the door and around to the side of the house Mica's room was on.

No Mica.

The window wasn't that far off the ground. If Mica had sneaked out in a fit of pique, at least she hadn't hurt herself in the drop.

If she'd gone out the window on her own...

Fear stabbed him in the heart.

What if Mica hadn't gone out that window on her own?

Sean leaned into the window, careful not to disturb any fingerprints in case someone had come in and taken Mica. "Call 911," he said.

Ava appeared in her daughter's doorway with her cellphone pressed to her ear. "My daughter is missing," she said. "Please send help."

Sean expanded his search, looking for any sign of

the little girl. If she had struggled, she might have lost a shoe or her hairbow.

He made a complete circle of the house and moved outward, performing a search of a one-hundred-foot radius of the structure.

Nothing.

He found Ava near Mica's window, wringing her hands, her face drawn and worried. "Where could she have gone?"

"Does she have any little friends in the neighborhood?" Sean asked. "Anyone she likes to visit on occasion?"

"She made a friend of Mrs. Tripley on the corner. She likes the woman's Yorkie." Ava started down the street.

Sean stopped her. "You need to stay at the house and be here in case Mica comes back or the police arrive. I'll go to Mrs. Tripley's. Which house is it?"

Ava pointed to the house on the corner by the stop sign. "She might not answer the door to a strange man. I'll call and let her know you're coming."

Sean ran down the road to the house and knocked loudly on the door.

An old woman opened it immediately. "Miss Swan told me about Mica." The old woman shook her head. "She hasn't been here. I'm so sorry I can't help. I hope you find her soon." Mrs. Tripley stared out at the darkening sky. "It's getting dark."

"Thank you, Mrs. Tripley." Sean said. "If you see her—"

"I'll hold her and call," Mrs. Tripley promised. "Good luck."

Sean returned to Ava's house where he found her pacing in the front yard.

A siren sounded nearby. Moments later, a police car pulled up to the curb, followed by three more. They lined the street, lights flashing.

Neighbors came out of their houses to see what all the commotion was.

Soon, the police had as many people as they could muster lined up with flashlights, each given a direction for a grid-search of the streets.

Sean put out the call to his friends. Soon, Coop, Tag, Gage, and Moose arrived with Emma, Leslie, Fiona and Jane. All four of Emma's brothers drove in from their ranch and joined the search.

Sean stayed close to Ava, slipping an arm around her when he thought she'd collapse from worry. The woman remained dry-eyed and tense, holding herself together by a thread.

"Is there anywhere in the neighborhood that Mica likes to play? A playground, playhouse, somewhere she likes to hide?" Sean asked. "If she was mad, she might be hiding somewhere."

Ava shook her head. "We walk to the playground every other weekend. It's three blocks away. I can't imagine she's gone that far by herself."

"She's a smart little girl. Don't underestimate her." Sean grabbed Ava's hand. "The police have your number if they need to get a hold of you. Let's go see if she made it to the playground."

"Leslie and I are going with you," Tag said. "The others are working the grid."

Ava led the way, taking the path she and Mica used to get to the playground. It involved going through an alley that connected to the street behind their house. Then she cut across a large baseball complex and, finally, came to the elaborate playground that had swings, a jungle gym and a fort with ropes, ladders and a slide.

"Mica!" Ava called out. "Mica, if you're here, please…let us know."

The four of them paused and listened.

"Mica," Sean yelled, "we're worried about you. Please, come out."

Again, nothing.

"She's not here," Ava whispered.

Sean wasn't ready to give up. "I'm going to check out the fort." Sean shot a glance toward Tag and Leslie. "Look inside the dugouts in the ball field."

Tag nodded. "On it." He and Leslie ran toward the dugouts.

Ava followed Sean. "She would have answered, if she was here."

"Maybe. Or she could be asleep or scared. You take the castle, and I'll take the ship." Sean started up the ladder on one side of the fort that was shaped like a pirate ship.

Ava climbed up into the castle.

When Sean reached the top, he shined his flashlight into ship. A tunnel led out of the ship to a rope bridge on one side and a tube slide on the other.

Movement caught his eye in the tunnel to the slide.

"Mica?" he called out softly.

He ducked low to get into the pirate ship and crawled over the tunnel, shining the beam of his flashlight in front of him.

The first thing he saw was a fat, purple unicorn and a pale arm clutching it.

"Oh, Mica, sweetheart. It's me, Mr. Decker," he said softly. "I found her," he called out loudly to Ava.

"Oh, thank God," she said. "Where is she?"

"In the slide tunnel. I'll bring her out." He focused on Mica. "Come with me, Mica. I'll take you home."

She shook her head. "I don't want to go home," she said.

"Why?"

A tear slipped from one of her eyes and made its way down her cheek. "You won't be there."

"Oh, Mica, whether I'm there or not, your mother loves you so very much. She was so worried about you."

"She doesn't love me."

"How can you say that? Your mother loves you very much."

"She doesn't want me to have a daddy." Mica sniffed.

"Sweetheart, your mother doesn't want you to have a daddy who doesn't love you."

Mica's eyes widened. "But you love me, don't you?" Her brow dipped. "You said you did."

"And I do. I love you and your mother very much. But just because your mother didn't want to marry again, doesn't mean she doesn't love you." Sean held out his hand. "She would do almost anything for you."

Mica reached for his hand and let him pull her toward him. "Except give me a daddy. She wanted you to go away. I heard her say so."

Sean hugged her close to him. "She told me the same thing. She thought I didn't want to be your daddy and that I couldn't love you as much as she thinks you deserve. She didn't want you to be hurt."

"But she hurt me by sending you away." Mica buried her face in his shirt. "I love you, Mr. Decker. I want you to be my daddy."

Sean's heart squeezed so hard in his chest. To have a little human want him that much made him reevaluate his life. "I want to be your daddy, too."

"But Mama won't let you."

"I don't know about that." Ava's head appeared

over the top of the ladder. "Mr. Decker and I have come to an agreement."

Mica frowned and looked from Sean to Ava, and then back to Sean. "Agreement?"

"That's right," Sean said. "I agreed to love you as much as I love your mother."

"And I agreed to marry Mr. Decker and love him as much as I love you."

Mica's eyes rounded. "If you marry Mr. Decker...I get a daddy!" She flung her arms around Sean's neck. After a quick, hard hug, she crawled across the deck of the ship and hugged her mother. "I love you, Mama."

Sean edged his way over to the two. "Can we go home now?"

"Yes!" Mica said.

Ava backed down the ladder with Mica in front of her. Sean was last, jumping the last few feet to the ground.

Ava lifted Mica into her arms and held her for long moment before she looked up. "We need to inform the police that we've found her."

Sean already had his phone out and was dialing the number for the policeman in charge of the search.

They picked up Tag and Leslie on their way back. Halfway to the house, the rest of their friends found them and gathered around to hug Mica and Ava.

At Ava's home, the police closed out their report

and left, smiling and happy that the search had ended with a positive outcome.

After congratulating Ava on finding her daughter, the neighbors returned to their homes, promising to visit more often and get to know each other.

Sean's friends gathered on Ava's front porch, all talking at once.

Ava leaned close to Sean. "Could you get their attention for me?"

Sean cleared his throat. "Hey, the lady of the house would like to say something. Then I want to say something as well." Sean pulled her close to his side and nodded. "They're all yours." And in a tone only she could hear, he added, "As long as you're all mine." He'd found the woman of his dreams and the daughter he'd never known he wanted. Life didn't get better.

AVA'S CHEEKS heated at being the center of attention of so many people she didn't know that well. But she was so grateful to all of them and wanted them to know.

She smiled at the crowd of friends and family. "Thank you all for coming to help us find Mica." She hugged her daughter close. "I've never been so scared in my life. And you all came running when Sean called. I can't begin to know how to repay you for taking the time to come to my aid."

Ava glanced down at Mica. "Is there something you want to say to all these nice people?"

Mica nodded. Then a smile split her face, and she shouted, "I'm getting a daddy!"

"What?" Tag raised his hands, palms up. "And who might your daddy be?"

Ava turned with Mica toward Sean.

Sean beamed and flung his arms wide. "We're going to be a family."

Leslie was first to turn to Ava. "How did this happen, and I didn't get all the details first?" She winked and hugged Ava and Mica. "Auntie Leslie couldn't be happier for you, Mica. Sean will be a wonderful daddy for you."

Mica nodded. "I know. He passed the daddy test."

"The daddy test?" Tag asked.

"Yes. The daddy test," Mica said.

Ava chuckled. "And what is the daddy test?"

All the adults quieted to hear Ava's daughter's response.

"He read to me," Mica said. "Jimmy's daddy doesn't read to him."

Sean nodded. "I read to you the first night we met."

"He came to my Daddy Day at my school," Mica said. "Even though he wasn't my daddy then."

Ava laughed. "You should have seen him sitting on the floor drinking punch with the five-year-olds."

Tag laughed. "I'd have paid money to see that."

Mica continued. "He took me on a Ferris wheel and didn't let me fall off. And he found me when I ran away. That must mean he loves me." Mica leaned out of Ava's arms into Sean's and hugged him close. "I love my daddy."

Tag clapped Sean on the back. "Congratulations, man. I can't believe you came to your senses so fast. I thought for sure you'd be the hard case to crack when it came to a BODS match."

Sean slipped his free arm around Ava. "I thought so, too." He smiled down at her. "Then I met Ava and Mica."

"Well, we have a reason to celebrate! It's not too late to head over to the Ugly Stick Saloon. Then we can all crash at my ranch," Coop said. "I have plenty of room."

Ava shook her head. "I can't leave Mica. Not after what we went through."

"Bring her. It just happens to be family night at the Ugly Stick," Emma said. "I've seen other children come. The kids love the music and dancing."

"Besides I've been teaching Coop how to two-step," Emma added. "He promised to dance with me tonight."

Coop held up his hand. "I did promise to dance with her. I didn't promise not to break her toes."

His friends and Emma's brothers all laughed and piled into their trucks and SUVs.

Sean helped Ava pack a bag for her and Mica and

lock up the house. The drive out to the Ugly Stick Saloon took a good hour through Austin traffic and out into the country.

Ava leaned back in her seat and relaxed for what felt like the first time in the six years since her husband's death. She glanced over her shoulder at Mica, who was sound asleep in her booster seat, and sighed.

"You're not having second thoughts, are you?" Sean asked.

"I should be asking you that question." She glanced across the console at him. "It's a big commitment to take on a ready-made family."

"Not if it's right," he said. "And this is the most *right* I've ever felt in my life." He smiled at her. "And damned if I don't find myself having to eat my words."

"What words?" Ava asked.

Sean laughed. "I told Leslie a machine couldn't possibly match two people. That it was all luck and willingness to find a wife that made it work for Coop, Gage and Moose."

"And now?" Ava grinned.

"I'll post a testimony to the BODS magic. I'm sold on its ability to bring two people together."

Ava reached across the console for his hand. "I didn't believe it would work, either. And I really didn't want to date. Leslie talked me into it."

"Two unlikely people find love in a computer

program." Sean shook his head. "Sounds like one of those romance novels."

"I should write it." She stared out at the stars shining down on the Texas landscape. "I love happy endings."

"Me, too," said a sleepy voice from the back seat. "Are we there yet?"

Ava held Sean's hand all the way to the Ugly Stick, counting her blessings over every mile they passed.

Life didn't get better.

Unless…

"How do you feel about children?" Ava asked.

"I love Mica. Why?"

"No. I mean children," she said. "Mica's a child. Children implies more than one."

Sean's eyes widened. "I hadn't thought about it."

Mica clapped her hands. "I got a daddy, and now I'm going to get a baby brother!"

EPILOGUE

Coop and Emma arrived at the Ugly Stick in time to corral several tables close to the dance floor for their large group.

Emma had him up on the dance floor when Sean and Ava arrived with Mica. All in all, Coop held his own and held Emma through two songs before the band started playing a waltz.

He dragged Emma back to the table. "I'm not ready to waltz."

"But we've been practicing," Emma was saying. "You'll do fine."

"Nope. I'll two-step, but no waltz tonight." Coop hooked a chair with his foot and held it for Emma.

"Okay. But next time, for sure." Emma winked at Coop and dropped into the seat. "He did good on the two-step, didn't he?" she asked the others.

"For a bull in a china shop," Sean said, grinning.

"I'd like to see you do better," Leslie challenged.

"Ava, how are you at waltzing?" Sean stood and held out his hand.

"I haven't waltzed since I danced it in grade school, but I'm game to try." She glanced toward Mica.

Leslie put an arm around Mica. "Mica and I are having Shirley Temples. You two go dance."

Sean led her out on the floor to dance to *Perfect*, a beautiful song by Ed Sheeran.

Sean led her expertly around the dance floor.

"You fit me perfectly," he said. "You know this is going to be our song."

Ava smiled. "How appropriate. Perfect."

"Yes, you are," he said and twirled her around.

"Where did you learn to dance so well?"

He grinned sheepishly. "I met a woman who taught ballroom dancing. She was convinced she could teach anyone." Sean chuckled. "I was her biggest challenge."

Ava cocked an eyebrow. "Should I be jealous?"

He laughed out loud. "Only if you think you're in competition with a fifty-year-old married woman." Sean tilted his head a bit. "As a matter of fact, she was pretty hot for fifty."

"You're impossible," she said and smiled.

"And you're perfect."

The song ended, and they made their way back to the group of tables where the others were in a lively debate.

"What did we miss?" Sean asked.

Coop pointed to Tag. "We were just discussing the fact that Tag is the last of our group to try his luck with BODS."

"And after him, my brothers are in need of a little matchmaking." Emma gave a stern look in her brothers' direction.

"Oh, hell no," said her oldest brother, Ace. "I don't need a computer finding a woman for me. I can do that myself."

"Uh huh." Emma crossed her arms over her chest. "And when was the last time you went out on a date?"

Ace glared at her. "None of your business."

Emma gave a firm nod. "Exactly."

"Tag? What's your holdup?" Sean asked. "You were the one who talked all of us into giving BODS a try. Isn't it about time you found your match?"

"Yeah," Coop said. "You're up, Tag. No more stonewalling."

"Yup," Gage added. "Tag's the last man standing in our Billionaire Anonymous Club. It's about time he puts his money where his mouth is."

Ava frowned. "Wait? What? What do you mean, *Billionaire* Anonymous Club?"

Emma's brow wrinkled. "You didn't know?" She

cocked a brow toward Sean. "What name did you use in BODS?" she asked.

"Sean Decker," Sean admitted. "But she knows my real name."

Emma turned back to Ava. "And you don't know who Sean O'Leary is?"

Gage leaned forward. "He's only one of the most sought-after, eligible bachelors in the state."

"The man's loaded," Moose said. He reached over and patted Jane's leg. "This is rich. Sean's found the love of his life, and she's not after his money."

"Do you even know what a breath of fresh air that is?" Gage asked.

Ava turned to Sean. "What are they talking about?"

Sean wished they hadn't brought it up. He liked knowing Ava loved him for himself, not his bank account. But she'd find out soon enough. "I'm a billionaire," he said quietly, his brow furrowing. "I hope that doesn't make you change your mind about me."

"Is there anything else you haven't told me?" she asked, her eyes narrowing.

He shook his head. "No, that's about it."

Ava blinked several times. "Wow. I'm not sure how I'm supposed to react. I just agreed to marry a billionaire." She frowned. "Does that mean we're not going to live in my cottage?"

"That's completely up to you," Sean said. "If you

want to live in that little house, we'll live in that house. If you want a house on the French Riviera, we can live there. Me, personally, I prefer to live on my ranch, surrounded by hundreds of acres and very few people."

"And stars?" she asked, leaning into the crook of his arm. "I'd love to live somewhere I can see the stars."

"I knew you were the perfect match for me." He kissed her in front of everyone.

Mica clapped her hands. "Do I get a pony?"

"Yes, ma'am, you do," Sean said.

"We still haven't settled a time and place for Tag to join the ranks of BODS graduates," Coop said.

Sean looked across at his friend. "Didn't you say something about you working on something and weren't quite ready?"

Tag nodded.

"Got it all worked out?" Leslie asked.

He nodded again. "I believe so."

"Good. I'll see you in my office bright and early Monday morning to get your profile entered."

"I'll be there," Tag said.

"Oh, boy. I can't wait to meet the woman who knocks Tag off his feet," Gage said.

"Me, too." Coop grinned and rubbed his hands together. "This is going to be good."

"Epic," Moose agreed.

"Seriously, guys. You'd think BODS was a miracle

worker." Tag stood and held out his hand to Leslie. "Wanna show these goofballs how to do a real two-step?"

Leslie placed her hand in his. "You bet."

Coop leaped to his feet. "Emma?"

"I'm ready for more two-stepping, toe-stomping." She laughed. "Lead the way."

Emma's brothers fanned out in the saloon, looking for likely dance partners. Two of them hit pay dirt. Two struck out and landed at the bar, ordering beer.

"I'm glad I'm out of the dating scene," Sean said.

"You were barely in it for all of a week," Moose said. "That's pretty fast for someone to fall in love."

"And what about us?" Jane, his fiancée and former runway model asked. "Come on, you need to make it up to me by dancing."

"You're taking your life into your own hands, woman."

"I know. But you're the only one I'd let stomp on my feet. Do you know how much these legs are insured for?"

Moose nodded. "Yes, I do. And they're worth every penny."

Sean leaned toward Mica. "How would my little girl like to learn how to two-step?"

"Yes!" Mica jumped up from her seat, grabbed his hand and dragged him out to the dance floor.

He'd never seen himself as a family man, not after

the way his father had raised him. But he had a chance to make things right with his world by helping Ava raise this precious little girl.

He was the luckiest man in the world to have two beautiful girls in his life to love.

VOODOO ON THE BAYOU

CAJUN MAGIC MYSTERIES BOOK #1

New York Times & *USA Today*
Bestselling Author

ELLE JAMES

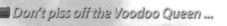
Don't piss off the Voodoo Queen ...

VOODOO
ON THE
BAYOU

A CAJUN MAGIC MYSTERY

NEW YORK TIMES & USA TODAY BESTSELLING AUTHOR

ELLE JAMES

CHAPTER 1

Bayou Miste, deep in the Atchafalaya Basin of southern Louisiana

June

Bound to a cypress tree, Craig Thibodeaux struggled to free his hands, the coarse rope rubbing his wrists raw with the effort. A fat bayou mosquito buzzed past his ear to feast on his unprotected skin. The bulging insect had plenty of blood in its belly—much more and the flying menace would be grounded.

What I wouldn't give for a can of bug repellent.

Craig shook his head violently in hopes of discouraging the little scavenger from landing.

The dark-skinned Cajuns who'd kidnapped him stood guard on either side of him, their legs planted wide and arms crossed over bare muscular chests. They looked like rejected cast members from a low-budget barbarian movie, and they didn't appear affected in the least by the blood-sucking mosquitoes.

"Hey, Mo, don't you think you guys are taking this a little too far?" Craig aimed a sharp blast of breath at a bug crawling along his shoulder. "I swear I won that card game fair and square."

The man on his right didn't turn his way or flick an eyelid.

Craig looked to his left. "Come on Larry, we've been friends since you and I got caught snitching apples from Old Lady Reneau's orchard. Let me go."

Larry didn't twitch a muscle, as if Craig hadn't uttered a word.

"If it will make you feel any better, I'll give you back your money," Craig offered, although he'd really won that game.

He'd known Maurice Saulnier and Lawrence Ezell since he was a snot-nosed kid spending his summer vacations with his Uncle Joe in the southern Louisiana town of Bayou Miste. He had considered them friends. Until now.

Granted, Craig had been back for less than a week after an eight-year sojourn into the legal jungles of the New Orleans court system. But his absence shouldn't be a reason for them to act the way they were. An odd sensation tickled his senses, as if foreshadowing something unpleasant waiting to happen. Sweat dripped off his brow, the heat and humidity of the swamp oppressive.

"Look guys, whatever you're planning, you won't get away with it." Craig strained against the bonds holding him tight to the rough bark of the cypress tree.

"Ah, *mon cher*, but we will." A low, musical voice reached out of the darkness preceding the appearance of a woman. She wore a flowing, bright red caftan with a sash tied around her ample girth and a matching kerchief covering her hair. Although large, she floated into the firelight, her bone necklace rattling in time to a steady drumbeat building in the shadows. Her skin was a light brown, almost mocha, weathered by the elements and age. Her dark brown eyes shone brightly, the flames of a nearby fire dancing in their depths.

Despite the weighty warmth of the swamp, a chill crept down Craig's spine. "Who's the lady in the muumuu?"

The silent wonder next to him deigned to speak in a reverent whisper, "Madame LeBieu."

Craig frowned and mentally scratched his head. Madame LeBieu...Madame LeBieu...oh, yes. The infamous Bayou Miste Voodoo priestess, a notorious mishmash of Cajun-Caribbean witchdoctor mumbo-jumbo and healer. No one really knew her background, but she was both feared and revered in the community. He studied her with more interest and a touch of unease. Was he to be a sacrifice in some wacky Voodoo ceremony?

"Are you in charge of these two thugs?" Craig feigned a cockiness he didn't feel.

"It be I who called upon dem." She dipped her head in a regal nod.

"Then call them off and untie me." Craig shot an angry look at the men on either side of him. "You've obviously got the wrong guy."

"Were you not de man what be goin' out with de sweet Lisa LeBieu earlier dis very evening?"

"Yes," Craig said, caution stretching his answer, as dread pooled in his stomach. He didn't go into the fact that Lisa wasn't so sweet. "Why?"

"I be Madame LeBieu and Lisa be *ma petite fille*. She say you dally with her heart and cast it aside." The woman's rich, melodious voice held a thread of steel.

Craig frowned in confusion. "You mean this isn't about the card game? This is about Lisa, your grand-daughter?"

"No, dis be 'bout you mistreatment of *les femmes*."

"I don't get it. I didn't touch her. She came on to me, and I took her home."

"Abuse not always takes de physical form. You shunned her love and damage her chakras. For dis, you pay."

Craig cocked an eyebrow in disbelief. "You mean I

was conked on the head and dragged from my bed all because I refused to sleep with your granddaughter?" He snorted. "This is a new one on me."

"Craig Thibodeaux, I know your kind." Madame LeBieu stuck a thick, brown finger in his face. "You be breakin' hearts all over, seein' all kinds of women, but got no love to show for it. You be showin' your loveless way for de last time." Madame LeBieu flicked her fingers, and the flames behind her leaped higher. Then, reaching inside the voluminous sleeves of the caftan, she whipped out an atomizer and sprayed a light floral scent all around him. The aroma mixed and mingled with the dark musty smells of the swamp's stagnant pools and decaying leaves.

"So you're going to douse me in perfume to unman me?" Craig's bark of laughter clashed with the rising beat of the drums. The humor of the situation was short-lived when the mosquitoes decided they liked him even more with the added scent. Craig shook all over to discourage the beggars from landing.

"Ezili Freda Daome, Goddess of love and all dat be beautiful, listen to our prayers, accept our offerings, and enter our arms, legs, and hearts." Madame LeBieu's head dropped back, and she spread her arms wide. The drumbeat increased in intensity, reverberating off the canopy of trees shrouded in low-hanging Spanish moss.

The pounding emphasized the throbbing ache in

the back of Craig's head from where Madame LeBieu's henchmen had beaned him in his room at the bait shop prior to dragging him here. The combined smells of perfume and swamp, along with the jungle beat and chanting nutcase made his stomach churn. The darkness of the night surrounded him, pushing fear into his soul.

Craig had a sudden premonition that whatever was about to happen had the potential to change his life entirely. Half of him wished they would just get on with it, whatever "it" was. The other half quaked in apprehension.

The Voodoo priestess's arms and head dropped, the drums crashing to a halt. Silence descended. Not a single cricket, frog, or bird interrupted the eerie stillness.

Craig broke the trance, fighting his growing fear with false bravado. "And I'm supposed to believe all this mumbo jumbo?" He snorted. "Give me a break. Next thing, you'll be waving a fairy wand and saying bibbity-bobbity-boo."

Madame LeBieu leveled a cold, hard stare at him.

Another shiver snaked down his spine. With the sweat dripping off his brow and chills racing down his back, he thought he might be ill. Maybe even hallucinating.

A small girl appeared at Madame LeBieu's side, handing her an ornate cup. She waited silently for the woman to drink. Craig noticed that his two former friends bowed their heads as the Voodoo lady sipped from the cup then handed it back to the girl. Clutching the cup as if it were her dearest possession, the child bowed at the waist, backing into the shadows.

With a flourishing sweep of her wrist, Madame LeBieu pulled a pastel pink, blue, and white scarf from the sleeve of her caftan, and waved it in Craig's face.

"*Mistress of Love, hear my plea.*

Help dis shameless man to see."

"You know I have family in high places, don't you?" Craig said. Not that they were there to help him now.

Madame LeBieu continued as though he hadn't spoken.

"*Though he be strong, his actions bold,*

his heart be loveless, empty, cold.

By day a frog, by night a man,

'til de next full moon, dis cunja will span."

Craig stopped shaking his head, mosquitoes be damned. What was the old lady saying? "Hey, what's this about frogs?"

"*A woman will answer Ezili's call,*

one who'll love him, warts and all."

"Who, the frog or me?" He chuckled nervously at the woman's fanatical words, downplaying his rising uneasiness. His next sarcastic statement was cut off

197

when Mo's heavily muscled forearm crashed into his stomach. "Oomph!"

"Silence!" Mo's command warned of further retribution should Craig dare to interrupt again.

Which worked out great, since he was too busy sucking wind to restore air to his lungs. All he could do was glare at his former friend. If only looks could kill, he'd have Mo six feet under in a New Orleans minute.

Madame LeBieu went on,

"He'll watch by day and woo by night,

to gain her love, he mus fight,

to break de cunja, be whole again,

transformed into a caring man."

"You didn't have to knock the wind out of my sails." Craig wheezed, and jerked his head in Madame LeBieu's direction. "She's the one making all the noise, talking nonsense about frogs and warts."

Mo's face could have been etched in stone.

The old witch held her finger in Craig's face, forcing him to look at it. Then she drew the finger to her nose and his gaze followed until he noticed her eyes. A strange glow, having nothing to do with fire, burned in their brown-black centers. Madame LeBieu's voice dropped to a low, threatening rumble.

"Should he deny dis gift from you,

a frog he'll remain in de blackest bayou."

With a flourishing spray of perfume and one last wave of the frothy scarf, Madame LeBieu backed away from Craig, disappearing into the darkness from whence she'd come.

Craig's stomach churned and a tingling sensation spread throughout his body. He attributed his discomfort to the nauseating smells and the ropes cutting off his circulation. "Hey, you're not going to leave me here trussed up like a pig on a spit, are you?" Craig called out to the departing priestess.

A faint response carried to him from deep in the shadows. "Dôn tempt me, boy."

As soon as Madame LeBieu was gone, the men who'd stood motionless at his side throughout the Voodoo ceremony moved. They untied his bonds, grabbed him beneath the arms and hauled him back to the small canoe-like pirogue they'd brought him in.

Forced to step into the craft, Craig fell to the hard wooden seat in the middle. When the other two men climbed in, the boat rocked violently, slinging him from side to side. One man sat in front, the other at the rear. Both lifted paddles and struck out across the bayou, away from the rickety pier.

"So what's it to be now?" Craig rubbed his midsection. "Are you two going to take me out into the middle of the swamp and feed me to the alligators?" He knew these swamps as well as anyone, and the threat was real, although he didn't think Mo and Larry would do it.

Would they?

"No harm will come to you dat hasn't already been levied by Madame LeBieu," Mo said. Dropping his macho facade, he gave Craig a pitying look. "She done put de *gree gree* on you. Man, I feel sorry for you."

"Why? Because a crazy lady chanted a little mumbo jumbo and sprayed perfume in my face?" He could handle chanting crazy people. He'd represented a few of the harmless ones in the courtroom. "Don't worry about me. If I were you, I'd worry more about the monster law suit I could file against the two of you for false imprisonment."

"Going to jail would be easy compared to what you be in for." Larry's normally cheerful face wore a woeful expression.

The pale light of the half-moon shimmered between the boughs of overhanging trees. Craig could see they were headed back to his uncle's marina. Perhaps they weren't going to kill him after all. Madame LeBieu was probably just trying to scare him into leaving her granddaughter alone. No problem there. With relatives like that, he didn't need the hassle.

Besides, he'd been bored with Lisa within the first five minutes of their date. Most of the women who agreed to go out with him were only interested in what his money could buy them. Lisa had been no different.

The big Cajuns pulled up to the dock at the

Thibodeaux Marina. As soon as Craig got out, they turned the boat back into the swamp, disappearing into the darkness like a fading dream.

Tired and achy, Craig trudged to his little room behind the shop, wondering if the night had been just that. A dream. He grimaced. Dream, hell. What had happened was the stuff nightmares were made of. The abrasions on his wrist confirmed it wasn't a dream, but it was over now. He would heed the warning and stay away from Madame LeBieu's granddaughter from now on.

He let himself in through the back door, flexing his sore muscles. The room was a mess from the earlier scuffle, short-lived though it was. Craig righted the nightstand and fished the alarm clock out from underneath the bed.

Without straightening the covers, he flopped onto the mattress in the tiny bedroom. It was a far cry from his suite back home, but he'd spent so many summers here as a boy, the cramped quarters didn't bother him. He was bone tired from a full day's work, a late night date gone sour, and his encounter with Madame LeBieu. What did it matter whether the sheets were of the finest linen or the cheapest cotton? A bed was a bed.

"Just another day at the office." He yawned. It would be dawn soon and his uncle expected him up bright and early to help prepare bait and fill gas tanks in the boats they rented to visiting fishermen.

Craig closed his eyes and drifted into a troubled sleep where drums beat, witches wove spells, and frogs littered the ground. A chant echoed throughout the dream, "By day a frog, by night a man, 'til the next full moon, this curse will span."

What a crock.

* * *

PROFESSOR AND RESEARCH scientist Elaine Smith moaned for the tenth time. How the staff must be laughing. Brainiac Elaine Smith, member of Mensa, valedictorian of her high school, undergraduate, *and* master's programs, with an IQ completely off the scale...and she hadn't had a clue. Until she'd opened the door to the stairwell in the science building to find her fiancé, Brian, with his hands up the shirt of a bosomy blond department secretary, while sucking out her tonsils.

The woman had seen her first, broken contact, and tapped Brian's shoulder. "Uh, this is a little awkward." She'd twittered her fingers at Elaine. "Hi, Dr. Smith."

"Elaine, I can explain," Brian had said, his hands springing free of the double-D breasts.

Without a word, Elaine had marched back to the lab. She'd only been away for a moment. If the drink machine on the second floor had worked, she wouldn't have opened that door. Thank God she'd made this discovery before she'd been even more idiotic and married the creep.

She crossed the shiny white floor to her desk and ran her hand over her favorite microscope, letting the coolness of the metal seep into her flushed skin. With careful precision, she poured a drop from the glass jar marked Bayou Miste onto a slide. With another clean slide, she smeared the sample across the glass, and slid it beneath the scope.

The routine process of studying microorganisms calmed her like no other tonic. Her heartbeat slowed and she lost herself in the beauty of microbiology. She didn't have to think about the world outside the science department. Many times in her life, she'd escaped behind lab doors to avoid the ugly side of society.

"Elaine the brain. Elaine the brain." Echoes of children's' taunts from long ago plagued her attempts at serenity.

Elaine snorted. *Wouldn't they laugh, now? Elaine-the-brain, too stupid to live.*

A tear dropped onto the lens of the microscope, blurring her view, and the lab door burst open. She scrubbed her hand across her eyes before she looked up. She'd be damned if she'd let the jerk see her cry.

"Elaine, let me explain." Brian strode in, a sufficiently contrite expression on his face.

He'd probably practiced the expression in the mirror to make it look so real. Elaine wasn't buying it. She forced her voice to be flat and disinterested. "Brian, I'm busy."

"We have to talk."

"No...we don't." She turned her back to him, her chest tight and her stomach clenching.

"Look, I'm sorry." Brian's voice didn't sound convincing. "It's just...well...ah, hell. I needed more."

Her mouth dropped open and she spun to face him. "More what? More women? More conquests? More sex in the hallways?"

He dug his hands in his pocket and scuffed his black leather shoe on the white tile. When he looked up, a corner of his mouth lifted and his gray eyes appeared sad. "I needed to know I was more important than a specimen, that I was wanted for more than just a convenient companion."

"So you made out with a secretary in the stairwell?"

"She at least pays attention to me." When she spun away, he grabbed her arm. "I should have broken our engagement first, but every time I tried, you'd bury yourself in this lab." He ran a hand through his hair and stepped closer. "It would never have worked between us. I couldn't compete with your first love."

"What are you talking about?"

"Your obsession with science." He inhaled deeply and looked at the corner ceiling, before his gaze came back to her. "Face it, Elaine, you love science more than you ever loved me."

"No, I don't." Her denial was swift, followed closely by the thought *'Do I?'*

He crossed his arms over his chest and stood with his feet spread slightly. "Then say it."

"Say what?"

"Say, I love you." He stood still waiting for her response.

She summoned righteous indignation, puffed out her chest and prepared to say the words he'd asked for. She opened her mouth, but the words stuck in her throat like a nasty-tasting wad of guilt. Instead of saying anything, she exhaled.

Had she ever really loved Brian? She studied his rounded face and curly blond hair. He had the geek-boy-next-door look, and he'd made her smile on occasion. She'd enjoyed the feeling of having someone to call her own, and to fill the lonely gap in her everyday existence. She hadn't had anyone in her life, no one to turn to since her parents had died four years ago. Having grown up too smart to fit in with kids her own age, she'd missed the much needed education only peers could provide and she didn't have any close friends. Had she wanted too much from Brian?

Had she really loved him? After all the years of living in relative isolation from any meaningful relationships, was she even capable of feeling love?

Her chest felt as empty as her roiling stomach. He was right. She couldn't say she loved him when she knew those words were a lie. And as much as she didn't like conflict, she disliked lying more.

How long had she been deluding herself into thinking they were the perfect couple?

"It's no use, Elaine. Our marriage would be a huge mistake. The only way you'd notice me is if I were a specimen under your microscope. It's not enough. I need more. I need someone who isn't afraid to get out and experience the world beyond this lab."

He turned and walked out, leaving a quiet room full of scientific equipment—and one very confused woman.

Afraid to get out? She glanced around the stark clean walls of the laboratory, the one place she could escape to when she wanted to feel safe.

Dear God, why can't I be like normal people? Brian was right. She felt more comfortable behind the lab door than in the world outside.

When she stared down at the litter of items on the table, blinking to clear the tears from her eyes, she spied the jar labeled Bayou Miste. The container had come to her in the mail, an anonymous sample of Louisiana swamp water. She stood, momentarily transfixed by the sight of the plain mason jar, a strange thrumming sound echoing in her subconscious, almost like drums beating. Probably some punk in the parking lot with his woofers too loud.

With an odd sense of fate, she leaned over the microscope, dried her tear from the lens with a tissue, and studied the slide. Her skin tingled and her heartbeat amplified. Here was her opportunity to get away from the lab.

She could help solve the pollution problems of an ecosystem, even if she couldn't solve the microcosm of her love life.

Read Voodoo on the Bayou Now

ABOUT THE AUTHOR

ELLE JAMES also writing as MYLA JACKSON is a *New York Times* and *USA Today* Bestselling author of books including cowboys, intrigues and paranormal adventures that keep her readers on the edges of their seats. When she's not at her computer, she's traveling, snow skiing, boating, or riding her ATV, dreaming up new stories. Learn more about Elle James at www.ellejames.com

Website | Facebook | Twitter | GoodReads | Newsletter | BookBub | Amazon

Or visit her alter ego Myla Jackson at mylajackson.com
Website | Facebook | Twitter | Newsletter

Follow Me!
www.ellejames.com
ellejames@ellejames.com

ALSO BY ELLE JAMES

Iron Horse Legacy

Soldier's Duty (#1)

Ranger's Baby (#2)

Marine's Promise (#3)

SEAL's Vow (#4)

Brotherhood Protectors Series

Montana SEAL (#1)

Bride Protector SEAL (#2)

Montana D-Force (#3)

Cowboy D-Force (#4)

Montana Ranger (#5)

Montana Dog Soldier (#6)

Montana SEAL Daddy (#7)

Montana Ranger's Wedding Vow (#8)

Montana SEAL Undercover Daddy (#9)

Cape Cod SEAL Rescue (#10)

Montana SEAL Friendly Fire (#11)

Montana SEAL's Mail-Order Bride (#12)

SEAL Justice (#13)

Ranger Creed (#14)

Two Dauntless Hearts

Three Courageous Words

Four Relentless Days

Five Ways to Surrender

Six Minutes to Midnight

Hearts & Heroes Series

Wyatt's War (#1)

Mack's Witness (#2)

Ronin's Return (#3)

Sam's Surrender (#4)

Take No Prisoners Series

SEAL's Honor (#1)

SEAL'S Desire (#2)

SEAL's Embrace (#3)

SEAL's Obsession (#4)

SEAL's Proposal (#5)

SEAL's Seduction (#6)

SEAL'S Defiance (#7)

SEAL's Deception (#8)

SEAL's Deliverance (#9)

SEAL's Ultimate Challenge (#10)

Texas Billionaire Club

Tarzan & Janine (#1)

Something To Talk About (#2)

Who's Your Daddy (#3)

Love & War (#4)

Ballistic Cowboy

Hot Combat (#1)

Hot Target (#2)

Hot Zone (#3)

Hot Velocity (#4)

Cajun Magic Mystery Series

Voodoo on the Bayou (#1)

Voodoo for Two (#2)

Deja Voodoo (#3)

Cajun Magic Mysteries Books 1-3

Billionaire Online Dating Service

The Billionaire Husband Test (#1)

The Billionaire Cinderella Test (#2)

The Billionaire Bride Test (#3)

The Billionaire Daddy Test (#4)

The Billionaire Matchmaker Test (#5)

SEAL Of My Own

Navy SEAL Survival

Conquests

Smokin' Hot Firemen

Love on the Rocks

Protecting the Colton Bride

Protecting the Colton Bride & Colton's Cowboy Code

Heir to Murder

Secret Service Rescue

High Octane Heroes

Haunted

Engaged with the Boss

Cowboy Brigade

Time Raiders: The Whisper

Bundle of Trouble

Killer Body

Operation XOXO

An Unexpected Clue

Baby Bling

Under Suspicion, With Child

Texas-Size Secrets

Cowboy Sanctuary

Lakota Baby

Dakota Meltdown

Beneath the Texas Moon

Made in the USA
Columbia, SC
20 January 2022

54532543R00124